PRAISE FOR *Cormac McCarthy*

"[McCarthy] puts most other American writers to shame. [His] work itself repays the tight focus of his attention with its finely wrought craftsmanship and its ferocious energy." —*The New York Times Book Review*

"McCarthy is a master stylist, perhaps without equal in American letters. . . . In [his] hands, everything is done with consummate skill—a kind of maximalism with precision crafting." —*Village Voice*

"No other novelist in America seems to have looked the work of Faulkner in the eye without blinking and lived to write in his spirit without sounding like a parody of the master." —*Dallas Morning News*

"A master in perfect command of his medium." —*Washington Post Book World*

"A true American original." —*Newsweek*

"Mr. McCarthy has the best kind of Southern style, one that fuses risky eloquence, intricate rhythms and dead-to-rights accuracy." —*The New York Times*

"McCarthy is a born narrator, and his writing has, line by line, the stab of actuality." —Robert Penn Warren

Cormac McCarthy

THE ORCHARD KEEPER

The novels of the American writer Cormac McCarthy have received a number of literary awards, including the Pulitzer Prize, the National Book Award, and the National Book Critics Circle Award. His works adapted to film include *All the Pretty Horses, The Road,* and *No Country for Old Men*—the latter film receiving four Academy Awards, including the award for Best Picture.

INTERNATIONAL

THE
ORCHARD
KEEPER

Cormac McCarthy

Vintage International

VINTAGE BOOKS

A DIVISION OF PENGUIN RANDOM HOUSE LLC

NEW YORK

FIRST VINTAGE INTERNATIONAL EDITION, FEBRUARY 1993

Library of Congress Cataloging-in-Publication Data
McCarthy, Cormac, 1933–
The orchard keeper / Cormac McCarthy.—1st Vintage
International ed.
p. cm.
Vintage International Trade Paperback ISBN: 978-0-679-72872-6
eBook ISBN: 978-0-307-76250-4
I. Title.
PS3563.C33707 1993
813'.54—dc20 92-56360
CIP

Author photograph © Marion Ettlinger

Manufactured in the United States of America

44th Printing

The Orchard Keeper

The tree was down and cut to lengths, the sections spread and jumbled over the grass. There was a stocky man with three fingers bound up in a dirty bandage with a splint. With him were a Negro and a young man, the three of them gathered about the butt of the tree. The stocky man laid aside the saw and he and the Negro took hold of the piece of fence and strained and grunted until they got the log turned over. The man got to one knee and peered into the cut. We best come in this way, he said. The Negro picked up the crosscut and he and the man began sawing again. They sawed for a time and then the man said, Hold it. Goddamn, that's it again. They stopped and lifted the blade from the cut and peered down into the tree. Uh-huh, said the Negro. It sho is now, ain't it?

The young man came over to see. Here, said the man, look sideways here. See? He looked. All the way up here? he said. Yep, the man said. He took hold of the twisted wrought-iron, the mangled fragment of the fence, and shook it. It didn't shake. It's growed all through the tree, the man said. We cain't cut no more on it. Damned old elum's bad enough on a saw.

The Negro was nodding his head. Yessa, he said. It most sholy has. Growed all up in that tree.

I

For some time now the road had been deserted, white and scorching yet, though the sun was already reddening the western sky. He walked along slowly in the dust, stopping from time to time and bobbling on one foot like some squat ungainly bird while he examined the wad of tape coming through his shoesole. He turned again. Far down the blazing strip of concrete a small shapeless mass had emerged and was struggling toward him. It loomed steadily, weaving and grotesque like something seen through bad glass, gained briefly the form and solidity of a pickup truck, whipped past and receded into the same liquid shape by which it came.

He swung his cocked thumb after it in a vague gesture. Little fans of dust scurried up the road shoulder and settled in his cuffs.

Go on, damn ye, he said to the fleeting mirage. He took out his cigarettes and counted them, put them back. He turned his head to the sun. Won't be no use after dark, he said. Windless silence, not even a rustle from the dusty newsprint and candypapers pressed furtively into the brown wall of weeds at the road edge.

Further on he could see the lights of a filling station, some buildings. Maybe a fork where the traffic slowed. He jerked his thumb at a trailer truck as it whined past, sucking up dust and papers in its wake, watched it wrench the trees farther up the road.

You wouldn't pick up Jesus Christ, would you, he asked, rearranging his hair with his fingers.

When he got to the filling station he had a long drink of water and smoked one of the cigarettes. There was a grocery store adjoining and he wandered in, cruising with a slithery sound up and down the aisles of boxes and cans and filling his pockets with small items—candy bars, a pencil, a roll of adhesive tape . . . Emerging from behind some cartons of toilet paper he caught the storekeep eying him.

Say now, he said, you don't have any, uh—his eyes took a quick last inventory—any tire pumps, do ye?

They ain't in the cake rack, the man said.

He looked down at a jumbled mound of bread and cakes, quietly lethal in their flyspecked cellophane.

Over here—the storekeep was pointing. In a crate at the back end of the counter were jacks, pumps, tire tools, an odd posthole digger.

Oh yeah, he said. I got em now. He shuffled over and fumbled among them for a few minutes.

Them ain't the kind I was lookin for, he told the storekeep, making for the door now.

What kind was that? the man asked. I didn't know they was but one kind.

No, no, he said, musing, standing just short of the door, rubbing his lower lip. He was inventing a new tire pump. Well, he said, they got a new kind now you don't have to pump up and down thisaway (pumping) but what's got a kind of *lever* handle you go at like this (pumping, one hand).

That a fact, said the storekeep.

Bet it is, he said. Makes it a whole lot easier on a feller too.

What kind of car you drivin? the storekeep wanted to know.

Me? Why I got me a new Ford. Brand-new thirty-four, V-eight motor. Scare you jest to set in it . . .

Lots of tire trouble though, hmm?

Well . . . no, jest this one time is the only first time I ever had me any tire trouble . . . Well, I better . . . say now, how fer is it to Atlana?

Seventeen mile.

Well, I reckon I better get on. We'll see yins.

Come back, the storekeep said. Shore hope you get your tire blowed up. It would be a sight easier with a pump.

But the screendoor flapped and he was outside. Standing on the store porch he studied the hour. The sun was already down. A cricket sounded and a squadron of bullbats came up out of the smoldering west, high on pointed wings, harrying the dusk.

There was a car pulled in at the filling station. He cussed the storekeep for a while, then walked back down and had another drink of water. From his pocket he produced a candy bar and began munching it.

In a few minutes a man came from the restroom and passed him, going to the car.

Say now, he said. You goin t'wards town?

The man stopped and looked around, spied him

propped against an oil drum. Yeah, he said. You want a ride on in?

Why now I shore would preciate it, he said, shuffling toward the man now. My daughter she's in the hospital there and I got to get in to see her tonight . . .

Hospital? Where's that? the man asked.

Why, the one in Atlana. The big one there . . .

Oh, said the man. Well, I'm jest goin as fer as Austell. How fer's that?

Nine mile.

Well, you don't care for me to ride that fer with ye, do ye?

Be proud to hep ye out that fer, said the man.

Coming into Atlanta he saw at the top of a fence of signs one that said KNOXVILLE 197. The name of the town for which he was headed. Had he been asked his name he might have given any but Kenneth Rattner, which was his name.

East of Knoxville Tennessee the mountains start, small ridges and spines of the folded Appalachians that contort the outgoing roads to their liking. The first of these is Red Mountain; from the crest on a clear day you can see the cool blue line of the watershed like a distant promise.

In late summer the mountain bakes under a sky of pitiless blue. The red dust of the orchard road is like powder from a brick kiln. You can't hold a scoop of it in your hand. Hot winds come up the slope from the valley like a rancid breath, redolent of milkweed, hoglots, rotting vegetation. The red clay banks along the road are crested with withered honeysuckle, peavines dried and sheathed in dust. By late July the corn patches stand

parched and sere, stalks askew in defeat. All greens pale
and dry. Clay cracks and splits in endless microcataclysm
and the limestone lies about the eroded land like schools
of sunning dolphin, gray channeled backs humped at the
infernal sky.

In the relative cool of the timber stands, possum grapes
and muscadine flourish with a cynical fecundity, and the
floor of the forest—littered with old mossbacked logs,
peopled with toadstools strange and solemn among the
ferns and creepers and leaning to show their delicate
livercolored gills—has about it a primordial quality,
some steamy carboniferous swamp where ancient saurians
lurk in feigned sleep.

On the mountain the limestone shelves and climbs in
ragged escarpments among the clutching roots of hickories, oaks and tulip poplars which even here brace themselves against the precarious declination allotted them by
the chance drop of a seed.

Under the west wall of the mountain is a community
called Red Branch. It was a very much different place
in 1913 when Marion Sylder was born there, or in 1929
when he left school to work briefly as a carpenter's ap-
prentice for Increase Tipton, patriarch of a clan whose
affluence extended to a dozen jerrybuilt shacks strewn
about the valley in unlikely places, squatting over their
gullied purlieus like great brooding animals rigid with
constipation, and yet endowed with an air transient
and happenstantial as if set there by the recession of
floodwaters. Even the speed with which they were constructed could not outdistance the decay for which they
held such affinity. Gangrenous molds took to the foun-
dations before the roofs were fairly nailed down. Mud
crept up their sides and paint fell away in long white
slashes. Some terrible plague seemed to overtake them
one by one.

They were rented to families of gaunt hollow-eyed and darkskinned people, not Mellungeons and not exactly anything else, who reproduced with such frightening prolificness that their entire lives appeared devoted to the production of the ragged line of scions which shoeless and tattered sat for hours at a time on the porch edges, themselves not unlike the victims of some terrible disaster, and stared out across the blighted land with expressions of neither hope nor wonder nor despair. They came and went, unencumbered as migratory birds, each succeeding family a replica of the one before and only the names on the mailboxes altered, the new ones lettered crudely in above a rack of paint smears that obliterated the former occupants back into the anonymity from which they sprang.

Marion Sylder labored with hammer and saw until late September of that year and then he quit, knowledgeable in purlins and pole plates, and with his savings bought some clothes and a pair of thirty-dollar boots mail-ordered out of Minnesota, and disappeared. He was gone for five years. Whatever trade he followed in his exile he wore no overalls, wielded no hammer.

At that time there was a place in the gap of the mountain called the Green Fly Inn. It was box-shaped with a high front and a tin roof sloping rearward and was built on a scaffolding of poles over a sheer drop, the front door giving directly onto the road. One corner was nailed to a pine tree that rose towering out of the hollow—a hollow which on windy nights acted as a flue, funneling the updrafts from the valley through the mountain gap. On such nights the inn-goers trod floors that waltzed drunkenly beneath them, surged and buckled with huge groans. At times the whole building would career madly to one side as though headlong into collapse. The drinkers would pause, liquid tilting in their glasses, the structure would shudder violently, a broom would fall, a bottle, and the inn would slowly right itself and assume once more its normal reeling equipoise. The drinkers would raise their glasses, talk would begin again. Remarks alluding to the eccentricities of the inn were made only outside the building. To them the inn was animate as any old ship to her crew and it bred an atmosphere such as few could boast, a solidarity due largely to its very precariousness. The swaying, the incessant small cries of tortured wood, created an illusion entirely nautical, so that after a violent wrench you might half expect to see a bearded mate swing through a hatch in the ceiling to report all rigging secure.

Inside there was a genuine bar, purportedly of mahogany, that had been salvaged from a Knoxville saloon in 1919, done service in a laundry, an ice cream parlor, and briefly in a catacombic establishment several miles from Red Branch on the Knoxville road that failed early in its career due to an attempted compromise between graft and cunning. With the exception of two Doric columns of white marble set in either end the bar was of plain construction. There were no stools, and along the front ran a high wooden foot-rail chucked between wagonwheel hubs. Four or five tables were scattered about the room attended by an assortment of wrecked chairs, milkcases, one treacherous folding campstool. When the inn closed at night the proprietor opened the back door and swept all litter out into the yawning gulf, listening to the crash of glass on glass far below. The refuse collected there cascaded down the mountain to a depth undetermined, creeping, growing, of indescribable variety and richness.

One evening late in March the drinkers blinked in a sweep of lights on the curve, watched a glistening black Ford coupe pull up across the road. It was brand new. A

few minutes later Marion Sylder came through the door
of the inn resplendent in gray gabardines, the trousers
pressed to a knife edge, the shirt creased thrice across
the back in military fashion, his waist encircled by a
strip of leather the width of a whip-end. Clamped in his
jaw was a slender cheroot. On the back of his neck a
scarlike gap between sunburn and hairline showed as he
crossed to the bar.

There he propped one pebbled goat-hide shoe upon
the rail, took from his pocket a handful of silver dollars
and stacked them neatly before him. Cabe was sitting on
a high stool by the cash register. Sylder eyed the coins
briefly, then looked up.

Come on, Cabe, he said. We drinkin or not?

Yessir, Cabe said, clambering down from his stool.
Then he thought: Cabe. He studied the man again.
Wraithlike the face of the lost boy grew in the features
of the man standing at the bar. Say, he said, Sylder?
You the Sylder . . . you Marion Sylder, ain't you?

Who'd you think I was? Sylder asked.

Well now, said Cabe, don't that jest beat . . . Where
you been? Hey, Bud! Looky here. You remember this
young feller. Well now. How about this.

Bud shuffled over and peered up at him, grinned and
nodded.

Here, Sylder said, give these highbinders a drink.

Sure thing, Cabe said. Who's that?

Sylder gestured at the dim smoky room. They all
drinkin, ain't they?

Well now. Sure thing. He looked about him, uncertain as to how to proceed, then suddenly called out into
the tiny room: All right now! All you highbounders got
one comin on Marion Sylder. Better get up here and
get it.

. . .

When Rattner reached the road he stopped and lit a match by which to examine his shin. In that small bloom of light the gash in his leg looked like tar welling. Blood trickled in three rivulets past the black smear his trouser had made, deltaed, rejoined; a thin line shot precipitously into his sock. He let go the match and jammed his scorched thumb into his mouth.

Aside from the torn leg his elbow was skinned and stinging badly. A low strand of barbed wire had been his undoing. Now he pulled a handful of dried weeds, crumpled and struck a match to them. They crackled in quick flame and he hiked his trouser leg again. Wiping the blood away with his palm he studied the rate of flow. Satisfied, he patted the sticky cloth back against the wound and took from his front pocket a billfold. Holding it to the light he pulled out a thin sheaf of folded notes and counted them. Then he ripped the billfold open, scattering cards and pictures. These he examined carefully along with the insides of the ruined purse, then kicked them away and tucked the money into his pocket. The weeds had burned to a ball of wispy cinders, still glowing like thin hot wires. He kicked them away in a burst of dying sparks. Far up the road a pale glow hung in the night like the first touch of dawn. He had left Atlanta at ten . . . it could not be past midnight. He patted his leg once more, sucked at his thumb, and started off in the direction of the lights.

Jim's Hot Spot, the sign said in limegreen neon. He circled catlike among the few cars, peering in at their black insides and keeping one eye weathered to the door where in a dome of yellow light an endless whirlpool of insects aspired. He came past the last empty car to the door and by this light checked his furrowed leg once again and then made his entrance.

. . .

The little coupe could be seen leaving or entering the Sylder place at strange hours, or in the heat of the day parked glistening and incongruous before the house, sleekly muscled and restless-looking as a tethered racehorse. Saturday evenings he collected parcels of townward-walking boys in new overall pants from the roadside as you might gather hounds the morning after a hunt—them leaping awkwardly in, riding solemnly or whispering hoarsely one to another until they gained speed. Sylder could feel their breath on his neck—those in the rear, wedged in like crated chickens—as they peered over his shoulder. A long silence as they watched the needle vanquish the numerals on the dial in a slow arc to hover briefly at 80 on the last and long straight stretch before reaching the city limits. Sometimes one of them would venture a question. He always lied to them. Company itself don't know how fast she'll go, he'd say. They plannin to take one over to the Sahary Desert to find out.

At Gay or Market he would pull to the curb and yell: One stop! and watch them erupt from the car like circus clowns—five, six, as many as eight of them, all bound for the show, farmboys with no more farm than some wizened tomato plants and a brace of ravenous hogs. In the rearview mirror he could see them watching the car scoot away, hovering and bobbing on the sidewalk like a flock of curious birds.

Sundays the Knoxville beer taverns were closed, their glass fronts dimmed and muted in sabbatical quietude, and Sylder turned to the mountain to join what crowds marshaled there beyond the dominion of laws either civil or spiritual.

Jack the Runner's mouth was blue, his tongue blueblack as a chow's. At the table by the door of the Green

Fly Inn he sipped blackberry wine from a liniment
bottle.

Where'd you leave em? Sylder was asking.

Ahh, Jack gurgled. Over on mountain.

You're on the mountain now, Sylder said.

Over, Jack emphasized. Hen'son Valley Road.

Henderson Valley Road? Whereabouts?

Top o mountain, like I tol ye . . .

You reckon he's tellin us right? June asked.

Sylder looked from him to the runner again. Jack
studied a huge and evil-looking cigar he had found in
his shirtpocket and fell to turning it against his tongue
with drunken singlemindedness. Yeah, Sylder said. Most
likely he is.

Right feisty, Jack was saying, holding now the cigar
at arm's length. A loop of spittle woggled mucously
from its underside. Right feisty.

Caught in the yellow glare of the headlights they had
the temporarily immobilized look of wildlife, deer perhaps, frozen in attitudes of surprise predicating imminent
flight. Sylder drove past and up the mountain.

Ain't you goin to stop? June asked.

Comin back, Sylder said. Behind em, like I was goin
their way. I never figured they'd be headed wrong. Way
they're goin, through Sevierville, it's near thirty mile.

Between them in the crevice of the seat nestled a mason
jar of whiskey. Sylder heard the skirling tin sound of
the lid being unscrewed and he reached out his hand for
June to pass the jar. Moths loomed whitely before the
windshield, incandesced, dusted the glass with mica. A
ballet of gnats rioted in the path of the headlights. He
drank and handed the jar back. Under the black hood
the motor hummed its throaty combustions.

Sylder thought about old man Tipton saying it wasn't

sensible as any fool could see that with the pistons going on an angle like that—lop-ass-sided, he'd said—they were bound to wear through on one side. Pistons were supposed to go up and down. Street's are full of em, he said, if it's any comfort to know you wadn't the only one took.

They turned at the quarry and came back down the mountain coasting silently, the tires making a soft slapping sound at the cracks in the asphalt. When the lights picked them up they began to group and sidle to the ditch as cows will. Sylder brought the coupe to a stop slowly alongside of them.

Howdy, said June right into the ear of the girl on the outside. You-all need a ride?

The other one was standing next to her then. They looked at each other and the first one said, Thank ye, I reckon we can make it all right. The boy hung back behind them. Across June's shoulder Sylder could see him looking not at them or at the women either, but at the car.

How fer ye goin? June wanted to know.

The two exchanged glances again. This time the taller one spoke up. We jest goin down the road a piece, she explained.

Tell her let's all go down the road for a piece, Sylder suggested.

What? the short one said. Then the boy piped up and they both turned to glare at him.

How fer is it to Knoxville? That was his question.

Knoxville? June couldn't believe it. You say Knoxville? Why you-all cain't *walk* to Knoxville. It's twenty mile or better—ain't it, Marion?

A groan went up from the travelers. Sylder was already motioning him out the door.

Here, June said, climbing out. You'ns get in here. We goin to Knoxville, proud to hep ye out.

Sylder presented them each with a welcoming smile as they climbed in and studied each in turn his face under the domelight.

He dropped into the Hopper—the steep twin fork road—without braking. The little one between him and Tipton squealed once and then hushed with her hand clapped over her mouth as they swerved across the pike and shot out into blackness, the lights slapping across the upper reaches of trees standing sharply up the side of the hollow. The coupe dropped, squatted for a moment in the gravel of the lower road, sprang again and slithered away obliquely with the exhaust bellowing from the cutout and gravel popping and rattling in the woods like grapeshot.

The one in the back was making small sobbing noises. No one spoke for a few minutes and then the little one said, Where's this go?

Goes to the gettin pla . . .

Town, June broke in. Goes to town. Shorter this way. He thought she seemed to have edged closer to Sylder although she turned and was talking to him. He saw Sylder's hand greenly phosphorescent under the dashlights pulling out the choke.

They reached the first bridge before it began to sputter enough for her to notice. Above here the road began to climb again and Sylder let it buck a time or two before he shifted to second. She didn't move her leg. He was watching her out of the corner of his eye, her sitting forward on the seat and peering out intensely at the unfamiliar night. A moth whipped beneath the windscreen, brushed her cheek. He cranked the glass in a turn. When the car bucked again she flinched and asked what was wrong.

He started to tell her the generator was out of water but thought about the boy in the back seat. No word from him at all. The tall one in the back had leaned forward, breathing in Tipton's collar and fixing the windshield with a look grim and harassed as if contemplating one desperate leap at the black passing night country.

Vapor lockin, he said finally. Overheats on these hills and you have to stop and let her cool off.

She looked at him and then looked away again, not saying anything. A phantom rabbit froze in the headlights, rolled one white eye, was gone. June was talking to her in a low voice, her still looking straight ahead, saying nothing. The one in the rear had sat back. No sound from her. In the mirror Sylder could see half a head dark and bushy in silhouette as a bear's. He recognized the smell then. A tepid odor of urine, musty-sweet, circulated on the air now as they slowed.

They jerked around the last curve below the pine thicket and shuddered to a stop in front of the Olive Branch Negro Baptist Church. Sylder switched off the ignition. I guess that's all she wrote, he said.

He opened the door and started to get out when he felt her hand on his leg. He stopped and turned.

Not him, she said. Not the other one.

No, he said. O.K. Come on.

He switched off the lights and then they were gone, negated in the sudden darkness.

Marion, June whispered hoarsely. Hey, Marion?

From his porch Arthur Ownby had watched them pass and now he heard the slam of the car door up the road where they had stopped. It had begun to rain. A yellow haze in the woods flicked out. He could hear low voices, near-sounding on the warm night air. With one foot he tapped out the time of some old ballad against the corner post of the porch. From under the brim of the roof he studied the movements of stars. A night for meteors tonight. They cannonaded the towering hump of Red Mountain. Rain falling now from a faultless sky. A girl's laugh on the road. He remembered her sitting high on the wagon seat Sunday morning that the mule broke wind in his ear while he unhooked the singletree and he stove two fingers in on a rib and it never even flinched. Late hours for an old man. Arthur Ownby had watched from his porch. He dozed.

When the boy came past on the road he looked up at the house on the sidehill, dark and abandoned-looking. He could not see the old man and the old man was asleep.

It was near daylight when they started back from Knoxville, a pale cold graying to the east.

Where'd you take her? Sylder asked.

June reached for the cigarettes riding in the visor. Goddamn she's ugly, he said. You know what she told me?

What's that, said Sylder, grinning.

That I was the nicest boy ever needled her. *Needled,* for God's sake.

Where at?

Huh?

Where'd you take her. You come down from the church but I never heard you come up. Where'd you go?

Ah. Up in the backhouse.

Backhouse?

Shithouse then.

Sylder was looking at him in amazed incredulity, acceptance and belief momentarily suspended, unable to picture it yet. He had one more question:

Standing up?

Naw, well . . . she sort of sat down and leant back

and I . . . she . . . But that was beyond his powers of description, let alone Sylder's imagination.

You mean to say you—Sylder paused for a moment trying to get the facts in summary—you screwed her in a nigger shithouse sittin on the . . .

Well Goddamnit at least I never took her in no Goddamn church, June broke in.

The coupe wobbled to a halt at the side of the road and Sylder collapsed against the door epileptic with laughter. After a while he stopped and said:

Was she the one that . . .

Yes, Goddamn you, she was the one.

Whooeee! Sylder screamed and rolled out the door where he lay in the wet morning grass shaking soundlessly.

The place was dimly lit and barnlike. A polished dance floor in which at the far end fell the reflection of the jukebox lights and those of the bar. Behind the bar a long mirror in which he was surprised to see himself, silhouetted in the doorframe, poised nimbly atop a stack of glasses. He came down and crossed the floor, limping slightly, and clambered up on the corner stool.

The bartender was sitting in a captain's chair reading a magazine. He folded it carefully and shuffled down to where the man was sitting.

Beer, Rattner said. His tongue swept his lower lip in anticipation. The bartender went to the barrel and drew off a schooner, flicked away the foam with a stick and brought it to him. He reached and tilted one side of the glass up and lowered his face into it; his lips sought the glassrim and fastened on it white and fat as leeches while under the yellowgray skin his throatcords jerked

spastically, pumping the beer down. He drank it all,
lifting the glass finally to drain it, and slid it back toward
the bartender, who had been watching with both fascination and disgust, as one might watch pigs mate.

Say now, that sure was all right. Yessir, jest believe
I'll have me anothern.

Ten cents, said the bartender.

He struggled with his pocket and came up with a
dime. You betcher, he said.

The bartender took the glass, gingerly, and refilled it.

Rattner had been gone for a year this time. He had
moved from Maryville to Red Branch, taken up quarters
in an abandoned log house with his wife and son, and
left there four days later with twenty-six dollars in his
pocket, alone and southbound in an empty L&N reefer.
An incident at the Green Fly Inn had been his windfall:

*The rear door through which Cabe swept the night's
litter had once given onto a porch that ran the width of
the building, supported by joists that were extensions
of the floor timbers and braced frugally with two-by-
fours angled up beneath them. On summer evenings the
drinkers gathered here, bringing with them their chairs
or cases or perching riskily upon the narrow railing like
roosting birds. Weather and termites conspired against
this haven and brought it to ruin. This was in 1933 then,
a hot summer night, that Ef Hobie came to the Green
Fly Inn. A prodigal return (Petros—Brushy Mountain—
eighteen months, illegal possession of liquor) that at-
tracted a great number of well-wishers. One by one they
retired through the rear door to take up their stations
on the porch. Hobie was a favorite and carried on a
running monologue of anecdotes. He was telling how
his old lady had loaned the family soupbone to Mrs
Fenner, who had cooked peas with it and ruined it,*

when a sharp dry crack issued from somewhere in the floor. It was a calm windless night, laden with heat, and the sound had an ominous quality about it. The talk paused a moment, resumed.

He came through the door and onto the porch, circumspectly, nodding across them all with diffidence, as if someone he knew might be there, beyond the railing itself and suspended mysteriously in the darkness, leaned against the doorframe and lifted the bottle to his mouth, his eyes shifting among them or when they looked closing or seeking again that being in the outer dark with whom only he held communion, smiling a little to himself, the onlooker, the stranger. The talk eddied and waned, but he offered neither comment nor question and after a while they ignored him. He came from the doorway and took a seat on the rail at the near end of the porch.

There was a long creaking sound like a nail being pulled and again the sharp detonation of strained wood giving way. There followed a dead and immobile silence during which the faces searched from one to the other uncertainly. A few began to rise and mill about, still not saying anything. Already they had begun to eye the narrow door, the one point of egress, weighing in their minds not so much numbers as tonnage and freight of men, calculating speed and congestion with the concern of traffic experts.

With the third report a section of flooring listed visibly.

Fellers, Ef started, rising himself, I think this here . . . But that was all, or as much as anyone heard at least. There ensued a single rush as of so many marionettes on one string being drawn in violent acceleration toward the door while above the noise of their retreat the joists popped like riflefire, snapping off in rackety succession, and the floor drooped in long and gathering undulations in their wake.

They hit the opening in one concerted mass and wedged there tight as a peg at the same instant that the far end of the porch came away, swung out from the building in a long swooping and not ungraceful arc.

Now from the knot of men clawing at the door single figures began to be sucked away in attitudes of mute supplication one by one down the dangling incline of the porch, gaining momentum among leaping cans and bottles, and dropping at last with wild cries into the pit below. A few caught at the rails and dangled there with stricken looks eying their fellows rocketing past into the night.

From within the building Cabe and a few others were trying desperately to untangle the mass that writhed in the doorway, resorting finally to taking hold of what limb presented itself and pulling until something gave. Thus the survivors came aboard bereft of one shoe, or both, or pants, or as with Hobie himself naked save for one half of a shirt. Until the frame of the door exploded inward carrying a good section of wall and they entered in a roil of bodies and crashing wood.

The porch had swung out and downward and now tottered for a moment on the strength of a single two-by-six before it too snapped and the whole affair slewed away with a great splintering sound. The figures clutching at the rails began to turn loose their holds, coming away by ones and twos like beetles shaken from a limb, and the entire wreckage descended in a slow tableau of ruin to pitch thunderously into the hollow.

The atmosphere inside seethed with an inchoate violence. Scared men, torn, unclothed and crushed, breathing loudly and sweating the sweat of subsiding panic, mounting outrage and indignity. One by one the fallen *were entering through the front door red with blood and clay and looking like the vanquished in some desperate encounter waged with sabers and without quarter. As they gathered strength from below two factions became apparent and they fell upon each other murderously and fought far into the night.*

Kenneth Rattner nursed a slashed hand as he squatted in a blackberry thicket below the inn and listened with quiet bemusement to the thrashings and curses of the victims. Someone had brought a light; he could see the flicker and sweep of it through the bramble wall. He pulled a kerchief from his pocket and tied it around his hand, pulling the knot to with his teeth. Then he worked his way carefully up to the road and started for home. Small groups of men were running up the mountain to the scene of disaster bearing lanterns and whispering hoarsely.

I got a job, he told her.

Praise God, she said. Whereabouts?

Greenville South Carolina, showing her the money now. Trainfare, he said. But he gave her five of the thirty-one dollars and they went to the store. He bought the boy an orange drink, lifted him onto the box where he sat holding it in both hands, watching. Mrs Eller was telling about it.

That Coy Tipton showed up here this mornin looked like he'd fell in a combine. Said they's three or four of em what lost their britches—I'd like to know how they done that my own sef—and when they clumb down in the holler to get em somebody had beat em there and stole their pocketbooks. She sat atilt in her rocker, fanned slowly with a church tract. Thiefs and drunks runs together I expect, she said. Ain't none of em but got what they's lookin for.

Mildred Rattner pinched from loaf to loaf across the

bread rack. When them as wallers in sin thinks they's gettin by with it, she said, that's when He strikes em in His holy wrath. He jest bides His time.

Kenneth Rattner stroked his stiffening leg, flexed his ankle. It was past midnight and people were coming in now. The bartender had abandoned his magazine and was moving nervously up and down the counter and filling glasses for the newcomers.

He drained the last of the beer and set the glass upon the bar. Hey, buddy, he called. Give us anothern over here. Hey, old buddy.

Saturday afternoons Marion Sylder would come in the store fresh-looking in starched khakis or overall breeches and go to the glass case and point out the socks to Mr Eller. Mr Eller would put the box on top of the counter and Sylder would hold up a pair and say: How much are these?

Quarter, Mr Eller would say. No change in price, still a quarter. All a quarter, ain't got no other kind.

Sylder would spin a quarter on the glass, take his socks and sit down on a milkcase in front of the stove. He would do them one at a time, taking off one shoe and sock and waving his bare foot about while he reached for the stove door, opened it, and swung in the old sock, holding it delicately. Then he would put on his fresh sock, lace up his shoe, and proceed to the other foot, the one with the big toe nailless and truncate. He was working in the fertilizer plant now. Noontimes he ate in the café the regular lunches, the thirty-cent specials with the lightbread that clove gluily to the palate, three slices with a thumbprint in the center served on a piece of waxed paper. Beans and fatmeat oozing grease into the greasy gravy that leaked down from the potatoes, a beaded scum of grease on the coffee, everything in fact lubricated as if all who ate there suffered from some atrophy of the deglutitive muscles which precluded swallowing. In late afternoon he returned, parked the coupe and crossed the gullied and wasted clay of the yard where an old tire still hung from the one knobby and leafless oak, and so into the unpainted house.

Within the hour he was out, washed and combed, blasting away the peaceful cricket sounds with the open cutout, tooling carefully down the corroded drive and onto the pike and gone.

To Happy Hollow or McAnally Flats. Mead's Quarry or Pennyroyal. Smoking shacks yellow with coal-oil light and areek with the sweetmold smell of splo whiskey.

Drinking, courting with ribald humor the country slatterns that hung on the city's perimeter like lost waifs; his favorites the ill-shapen: Wretha, white lisle uniform, thighs the dimensions of oiltuns. The too thin. A nameless one, bony rump that cut into his leg. Experimentally he wet a finger and cut a white streak on the grime of her neck.

Some nights he made it to the Green Fly Inn and rocked away with those old boozers to the last man, this affluent son returned upon them bearing no olive branch but hard coin and greenbacks and ushering in an era of prosperity, a Utopia of paid drinks.

He was hard-pressed now on eighteen dollars a week, who had spent that in an evening. He turned twenty-one in August.

The following Friday he lost his job at the fertilizer plant. Aaron Conatser needled him into a fight, and he fought, not out of any particular dislike toward Conatser, or even in any great anger, but only to get the thing over with, settled. Conatser was the only man in the plant his size and had been looking to try him.

He was on one knee with his arms locked around Conatser's neck when he heard Conatser's hoarse breathing stop. There was no sound in the shipping room and when he raised his head he saw that the men standing around them were looking past him at something else and knew before he turned that Mr Petree had joined the circle. Not the dock foreman, or even the supervisor, either of whom would have said Break it up. He turned loose of Conatser and stood. Conatser came up too, stretching his neck like a mute rooster, and put his hands in his back pockets with elegant indifference.

He licked at the trickle of blood from his nose, tasting it salty and metallic, and turned to see what the old man would have to say. But Petree spun on his square leather heel and stalked briskly back down the aisle, the shipping-room floor echoing his hollow footfalls among the tiers of bags.

The three or four men who had gathered to watch the fray dispersed in silence, faded or slunk away in the dark malodorous aisles, less brazen than the rats that nested beneath the pallets. He and Conatser stood glaring at each other for a small minute, breathing laboriously. Then Conatser turned his head and spat, looked once obliquely across his shoulder at him and sauntered away toward the dock.

The dock foreman came down just before quitting time and told him. I tried to put in a word for you, he said, but he wadn't hearing any.

Sylder doubted him but muttered a thanks anyway and started for the office.

Where you goin? he asked.

Get my pay.

Here, he said. Sylder turned. He was holding out the envelope toward him.

Sylder went to Monk's and drank beer till six or seven o'clock, and finally went home. By eight o'clock he had packed some clothes into an old cardboard grip and was sitting grimly behind the wheel of the little coupe with the headlights clearing out the night ahead and a narrow strip of asphalt numbered 129 slipping away beneath him like tape from a spool. He stopped once at a grill outside of Chote, drank two warm beers from coffeecups and bought cigarettes. In the mountains the road was thin and gravel and he slewed down the curves on drifting wheels. Once a bobcat stood highlegged and lanterneyed in the road, bunched, floated away over the roadbank on invisible wires. For miles on miles the high country rolled lightless and uninhabited, the road ferruling through dark forests of owl trees, bat caverns, witch covens.

He smoked continuously, cranking in the windshield to light a fresh cigarette from the old stub and studying in the glare of their union his shadowed muzzle in orange relief on the glass, watching the point of light fade when he exhaled and climb slowly up the dark mirror like a sun risen inexplicably by night as he turned the glass out again to let in the damp rush of air, the retired butt curving past the cowl to be swept away in a swift red arc. At Blairsville he filled up with gas and did not stop again after that. Out across the flats he could see the moon on the river curling under the black fall of the mountain, plating the riffles in chain-work, hordes of luminous snakes racing upriver over the sounding rocks. The air came cool and damp under the windscreen.

He reached Atlanta some time after midnight but did not go into town. He pulled in at a roadhouse just short of the city limits and sat in the car for a few minutes flexing his eyelids. There were three or four other cars parked in front, dimly lustrous in the neon ambience.

He passed through a fanfall of moths under the yellow doorlight and inside. Above the heads of the dancers he could see himself hollow-eyed and sinister in the bar mirror and it occurred to him that he was ungodly tired. He skirted along the high booths lining the walls and got to the bar where he ordered and drank straight four shots of whiskey. He began to feel better. He was sitting with the fifth drink before him when sounds of breaking glass issued from the dance floor and he turned to see two men circling warily with clenched bottles. A huge figure hulked up from the end of the bar and shuffling out through the gathering spectators seized the combatants one in each hand by the belts and turkey-walked them out the door, them stepping high, unprotesting, their bottles dangling idly.

Whooee! see them turkeys trot, a man down the bar called out. The bouncer came back down the floor wearily, not smiling, faded again into the shadows. Sylder tossed off the drink, watched the blur of faces for a few minutes, not even high on the liquor, just feeling waves of fatigue roll from him. He didn't even think he was mad any more. A few minutes later he left, wondering vaguely as he stepped into the air again why he had come here and where he thought he was going. Louisiana or anywhere else, his job had gone off the market December fifth 1933.

He walked out in the quiet darkness, across the gravel, limping just a little on the bad ground. He got to the car and opened the door.

By the phosphorous glow, more like an emanation from the man's face than from the domelight, Sylder froze, his hand batting at the air stirred by the outflung door. The face stared at him with an expression bland and meaningless and Sylder groped for some, not cause or explanation, but mere association with rational experience by which he could comprehend a man sitting in his car as if conjured there simultaneously with the flick of light by the very act of opening the door.

The mouth stretched across the lower face in a slow cheesy rictus, a voice said: You goin t'wards Knoxville?

—A strained octave above normal, the pitch of supplication.

Sylder's hand found the door and he expelled a long breath. What in the Goddamn hell you doin in my car, he croaked. Something loathsome about the seated figure kept him from reaching for it violently, as a man might not reach for bird-droppings on his shoulder.

The mouth, still open, said: I seen your plates, Blount County—that's where I'm from, Maryville. I figured you might be goin thataway. I need a ride bad . . . 'm a sick man. The tone cloying, eyes dropped to Sylder's belt as if addressing his stomach. It was not presentiment that warned Sylder to get shed of his guest but a profound and unshakable knowledge of the presence of evil, of being for a certainty called upon to defend at least his property from the man already installed beneath his steering wheel.

You're sick all right, Sylder said. Scoot your ass out of there.

Thanks, old buddy, the man said, sliding across the seat to the far door without apparent use of any locomotor appendages but like something on runners tilted downhill. There he sat.

Sylder leaned his head wearily against the roof of the car. He knew the man had not misunderstood him.

I knowed you wouldn't turn down nobody from home, the voice said. You from Maryville? I live right near there, comin from Floridy . . .

Sylder lowered himself into the car, the hackles on his neck rising. He looked at the man. I would have to put you out with my hands, he said silently, and he could not touch him. He slipped the key into the switch and started the motor. He felt a terrific need to be clean.

Shore is a nice autymobile, the man was admiring.

Swinging the little coupe through the rutted drive and out onto the paving he thought: He'll be a talker, this bastard. He'll have plenty to say.

In immediate corroboration the man began. This sure will help me out, old buddy. You know it sure is hard to get a ride nights.

Morning, Sylder muttered under the vehement shift to second.

—specially not much traffic and what they is folks won't hardly pick you up even . . .

Ah, Sylder thought, shouldn't have thrown that shift. He could see the knee out of the corner of his eye, cocked back on the seat, the man sitting half sidewise watching him.

—My mother been real bad sick too, she . . .

Sylder's hand moved in stealth from wheel to shift-lever, poised birdlike. The hand on the speedometer climbed with the hum of the motor.

—doctor's bills is higher'n . . .

His left foot dropped the clutch. Now. Under his

cupped palm the gearshift shot down viciously, quivered where a moment before the man's knee had been.

—so I shore do preciate it . . . The man went on, droning, his legs now crossed with an air of homey comfort, slightly rocking.

Sylder hung his elbow over the doorsill and leaned his ear to the rush of wind, the pockety rhythm of the open exhaust and the black road slishing oily under the wheels, trying to lose the voice.

No cars passed. He drove in almost a trance, the unending and inescapable voice sucking him into some kind of oblivion, some faltering of the senses preparatory to . . . what? He sat up a little. The man had not taken his eyes from him, and yet never looked directly at him.

You bastard, Sylder thought. It began to seem to him that he had driven clear to Atlanta for the sole purpose of picking up this man and driving him back to Maryville. His back hurt. I must be crazy, he said to himself, reaching in his pockets for cigarettes. This son of a bitch will have me crazy anyway. He jiggled one from the pack, spun it leisurely between thumb and forefinger to his lips. He had the pack in his other hand then riding the top of the steering wheel. I'll bet I don't make it, he wagered, don't reach it. His right hand having delivered the cigarette to his mouth was creeping slowly for the pack to put it away. It was halfway up the steering wheel when the voice, suddenly clear, hopeful, said:

Say, wonder could I get one of them from ye . . . (leaning forward, already reaching) . . . I run out a while back and ain't . . .

Sylder chuckled and straight-armed the pack at him. Sure, he said. Help yourself. He waited a few seconds,

listening to the paper rustle, the man getting the cigarette. He could feel him hesitate, the eyes turn on him.
Then the package came back.

Thanks, old buddy, the man said.

Sylder waited. The man didn't say anything more.
Waiting too. Sylder produced the matches with painful
deliberation. Catching up his knee to the underside of
the wheel he steered that way and with studied slowness
fumbled a match from the box and struck it. Shielding
the flame with his hands he lit the cigarette, then
dropped the dying match over his elbow into the slip-
stream boring past the open windwing and took the
wheel once more, exhaling luxuriously and repocketing
the matches. He waited.

Say, old buddy, I wonder if I could get a . . . why
thanks, thank ye.

The match scratched and popped. Sylder meditated in
the windshield the face of the man cast in orange and
black above the spurt of flame like the downlidded face
of some copper ikon, a mask, not ambiguous or inscrut-
able but merely discountenanced of meaning, expression.
In the flickery second in which Sylder's glance went to
the road and back the man's eyes raised to regard him
in the glass, so that when Sylder looked back they faced
each other over the cup of light like enemy chieftains
across a council fire for just that instant before the man's
lips pursed, carplike, still holding the cigarette, and
sucked away the flame.

They smoked, the heat of the night air moving over
them heavy as syrup. In the dark glass where the road
poured down their cigarettes rose and fell like distant
semaphores above the soft green dawn of the dashlights.

He stopped at Gainesville for gas which he didn't
need and went into the men's room taking the keys

with him. The man sat in the car. Inside, Sylder lit a cigarette, smoked it in long pulls and flipped the butt into the toilet. He splashed some cold water on his face and went out again, paid the sleepy-eyed attendant and got in the car. The man was sitting as he had left him. An unmistakable trace of fresh tobacco smoke hung on the wet air.

Dawn. Fields smoking where the mist shoaled, trees white as bone. The gray shrubbery hard-looking as metal in the morning wetness. Beads of water raced on the windscreen and he turned on the wipers, watched the arms descend in slow benediction, was mopping at the glass with the back of his hand when the right rear tire went out with a sudden hollow detonation and they flapped to a stop.

Later Sylder realized that the man had passed up one chance with the jack handle, had waited until he took the jack from under the car and handed it himself to the man to put in the trunk. And realized too that the man had only miscalculated by part of a second the length of time it would take him to bend and slam the hubcap back on the rim with the heel of his hand. So although he never saw it, had no warning, he had already made a half turn and started to rise when the jack crashed into his shoulder and slammed him into the side of the car. Something crashed alongside his head into the quarterpanel—he remembered that too, but couldn't know until later that it was the base of the jack. He didn't duck the second time either, but only slid down the door of the coupe when the man swung, sideways —he was watching him now—tearing a ragged hole in the metal. Then he was sitting on the ground, his head leaned back against the door, looking up, not yet outraged but only in wonder, at the figure above him, his arm trailing in the dirt like a shattered wing. But when the man jerked the shaft of the jack from the punctured door he reached up, slowly, he thought, and laid his hand on the jack and still slowly closed his fingers over it. The man looked down at him, and in the gradual suffusion of light gathered and held between the gloss of the car's enamel and the paling road dust he saw terror carved and molded on that face like a physical deformity. They were like that for some few seconds, he sitting, the man standing, holding either end of the jack as if suspended in the act of passing it one to the other. Then Sylder stood, still in that somnambulant slow motion as if time itself were running down, and watched the man turn, seeming to labor not under water but in some more viscous fluid, torturous slow, and the jack itself falling down on an angle over the dying forces of gravity, leaving Sylder's own hand and bouncing slowly in the road while his leaden arm rose in a stiff arc and his fingers cocked like a cat's claws unsheathing and buried themselves in the cheesy neck-flesh of the man who fled from him without apparent headway as in a nightmare.

Whether he fell forward or whether the man pulled them over he did not know. They were lying in the road, the man with his face in the dirt and Sylder on top of him, motionless for the moment as resting lovers. Something in Sylder's shoulder traveled obliquely down to his lungs with each breath to cut off the air. He still had one hand locked in the man's neck and now he inched himself forward and whispered into his ear:

Why don't you say something now, bastard? Ain't you got some more talk to spiel for us?

He was jerking at the man's head but the man had both hands over it and seemed lost in speculation upon the pebbles of the road. Sylder let his hand relax and wander through the folds of the neck until they arrived at the throat. The man took that for a few minutes, then suddenly twisted sideways, spat in Sylder's face, and tried to wrench himself free. Sylder rolled with him and had him then flat backward in the road and astride him, still the one arm swinging from his broken shoulder like a piece of rope. He crept forward and placed one leg behind the man's head, elevating it slightly, looking like some hulking nurse administering to the wounded. He pushed the head back into the crook of his leg, straightened his arm, and bore down upon the man's neck with all his weight and strength. The boneless-looking face twitched a few times but other than that showed no change of expression, only the same rubbery look of fear, speechless and uncomprehending, which Sylder felt was not his doing either but the everyday look of the man. And the jaw kept coming down not on any detectable hinges but like a mass of offal, some obscene waste matter uncongealing and collapsing in slow folds over the web of his hand. It occurred to him then that the man was trying to bite him and this struck him as somehow so ludicrous that a snort of laughter wheezed in his nose. Finally the man's hands came up to rest on his arm, the puffy fingers trailing over his own hand and wrist reminding him of baby possums he had seen once, blind and pink.

Sylder held him like that for a long time. Like squeezing a boil, he thought. After a while the man did try to say something but no words came, only a bubbling sound. Sylder was watching him in a sort of mesmerized fascination, noting blink of eye, loll of tongue. Then he eased his grip and the man's eyes widened.

For Christ's sake, he gasped. Jesus Christ, just turn me loose.

Sylder put his face to the man's and in a low voice

said, You better call on somebody closer than that. Then
he saw his shoulder, saw the man looking at it. He dug
his thumb into the man's windpipe and felt it collapse
like a dried tule. The man got his hand up and began
with his eyes closed to beat Sylder about the face and
chest. Sylder closed his eyes too and buried his face
in his shoulder to protect it. The flailings grew violent,
slowed, finally stopped altogether. When Sylder opened
his eyes again the man was staring at him owlishly, the
little tongue tipped just past the open lips. He relaxed his
hand and the fingers contracted, shriveling into a tight
claw, like a killed spider. He tried to open it again but
could not. He looked at the man again and time was
coming back, gaining, so that all the clocks would be
right.

The man had been dead for perhaps a quarter of an
hour. Sylder staggered to the car and sat on the runningboard, stared unblinking into the brass eye of the sun
ponderous and unreal on the red hills until he lost
consciousness.

Morning. Lying with his cheek in the dust of the
road he had a child's view, the jack looming like a fallen
tree and beyond that the man face-upward like a
peaceful giant composed for sleep. The rocks in the
road threw long shadows and the first birds were about.

Sylder had already started dragging the heavy body
off into the johnson grass and poison ivy when he heard
the sound of a motor somewhere on the curves behind
him. He stopped, then turned and started toward the
coupe again trying to run and dragging the carcass
behind him with one hand, stumbling, knowing halfway
there that he would never make it, that he had made a
mistake. So he didn't even open the door but dropped

the body as he reached the car, squatted over it, and gripping the underside of the runningboard for support jacked his feet up into the man's armpits and slid him toes up beneath the car for three-fourths his length just as a truck rounded the far curve and caught him struggling to his feet.

The sun was well up. Across the open country, the wale of pines shedding scarves of mist like swamp gases rising on the steamy air, some crows were hawking their morning calls. Sylder scooted from under the car, stood and was idly toeing out the drag-marks when the truck pulled alongside. He knew they would stop and already he began to think that he had done the best thing, that they would have seen the man inside, would insist on helping when they saw his . . . His arm: he snapped his head and two faces peering from the halted truck blurred and he looked down and saw the great smear of blood on his arm and dried and blackening on his shirtfront, was still looking at it sickly when a voice from the truck said:

Kin we hep ye?

He didn't look up for a second, caught in the pain of his wrecked shoulder raging now as if loosed by the voice from the truck cab, and not lost either to the irony of it. Then he raised his face to the curious sympathetic eyes watching him with a bland serenity that not even the bloody vision of himself could ruffle.

They were on the far side, he looking at them across the incline of the open turtledeck, so that even as he said *We* he thought: They can't see him. Yet he couldn't get his mind that far ahead, and even afterwards could not trace the possibilities on their separate courses. He reconciled the whole thing by this: that there was no way to keep them from getting out of the truck anyway.

So he said: We had a little accident, and thought Yes, they will get out anyway. These bastards will jest have to get out and see good.

The truck doors spread simultaneously like rusty wings and fell to in a rattle of glass uncushioned by any upholstery. They were a man and his son, the elder heavy and red, with creased skin, the younger a tall and thinner duplication. They came shuffling around the rear of the car with an air of infinite and abiding patience. Sylder turned slowly, his eye raking over the scene, trying to imagine what it looked like: the feet protruding solemnly from under the car, the car itself with the hole torn in the quarterpanel and in the door, the dent where the base of the jack hit and the jack lying in the road . . .

You hurt bad? the man asked.

Naw, Sylder grunted. The man was looking past him. What happent?

Car fell, Sylder said. No-account piece of a jack give way on me. He kicked at the handle.

The man eyed the strewn jack. Shore did now, didn't it, he said. Whew. Them things'r dangerous as a cocked gun. Always have maintained it. How about your buddy there? Nodding at the upturned feet.

Yeah, Sylder said to himself. How about him now. Then to the man: He's all right. Knocked the muffler down when she fell. Soon's he gets her wired back we'll be set. The man was moving around him; Sylder cut him off. Say, he said, tell you what you might do.

What's that?

Get your dead ass out of here, Sylder thought. He said: Well, you might carry me down to Topton, see a doctor. Durned arm's bleeding pretty bad.

Shore, said the man, I guess we might better at that. Looks pretty bad. You come on.

They started for the truck, Sylder behind them, herding them. He moved around to the cab, hung back till the older one got in, then stooped to one knee and spoke loudly to the corpse:

Listen, these fellers going to carry me in to Topton to the doc's. You come on when you get done . . . You all done? He rose and turned to the man sitting now in the truck, the motor already started. Listen, he said. He's about done, I'll jest go on in with him. You fellers go on, we'll be all right now . . . and thinking *Will you go now? Will you go?*

Well, the man said, leaning across the boy (wide-eyed, still silent, getting into the truck), you sure you okay now?

Sure, Sylder said, already waving to them. Much obliged.

You're more'n welcome, the man said. His face moved back, the boy nodded. The gears shifted with a grating sound and the motor died, hushed suddenly in the blue stillness of the broken day.

Sylder stood there listening to the tortured cranking of the starter and thinking: Ah, God. I should've knowed. That raggedy-assed son of a bitch ain't goin to . . .

But it did. The motor coughed a few times, then clattered to a low roar. The gears raked again and the truck pulled away sifting up dustspurs from the rear wheels and was gone almost instantly beyond the curve of the road.

They never seen the hole, Sylder said. They must never of even seen it. Then he thought: How in hell would they know how long it'd been there if they had?

He turned and made for the far side of the car, listing badly, staggerfooted, reeled at the rear bumper and collapsed into the trunk whacking his broken shoulder against the spare tire. There he sat for some minutes dazed and his mind threatening unconsciousness again.

Got to get the hell out of here, he said, shaking his head and wobbling to his feet. He steadied himself with one hand against the cool skin of the coupe, worked his way to the other side and squatted there above the brogans. He cursed them for a while, then took hold of one worn heel and bracing a foot against the running-board began to pull the man out. He tried not to look when the head emerged, then gave up and had a good look. The eyes were leaping from their sockets, an expression of ghastly surprise, the tongue still poking out. Sylder pulled him to the back of the car, got his hand in the shirt collar, lifting him bodily, and jerked him into the trunk. Only the legs dangled over the bumper and these he folded in after. Then he collected the jack and threw it in, dropped the lid, went to the switch for the keys and locked the trunk.

Night. The coombs of the mountain fluted with hound voices, a threnody on the cooling air. Flying squirrels looped in feathery silence from tree to tree above the old man sitting on a punk log, his feet restless trampling down the poison ivy, listening to Scout and Buster flowing through the dark of the flats below him, a swift slap slap of water where they ghosted through the creek, pop of twig or leaf-scuttle brought to his ear arcanely —they were a quarter mile down—and the long bag-throated trail-call again.

When Sylder turned the key, the handle, and swung the lid up, he didn't expect the stench that followed, poured out upon him in a seething putrid breath. He didn't even have time to step back. The spume of vomit roiled up from the pit of his stomach and he staggered away through the brush and saplings, retching, finally falling to his knees and heaving in dry and tortured paroxysms. After a while it stopped. He sat there for a long time with the sour green taste of bile in his mouth, lightheaded, trying to make himself believe that he could go back and do what he had to. He stood up and smoked a cigarette.

A smell of honeysuckle came up the mountain, wafted on the cooling updrafts. Treefrogs and crickets called. A whippoorwill. Abruptly the yap of hounds treeing. His shoulder was pounding again and the cast had begun to cut into his armpit. He still couldn't take a full breath. He started back, the Ford outlined through the silhouettes of trunks and branches like a night animal feeding, a shape massive and bovine. At the rear bumper he sniffed tentatively, then resolutely reached into the foul darkness and clamped his hand over one leg. Turning his head he stepped away, hearing the rasp and slide of it following and the thump and jar when it fell to the ground. Past the car, edging along the screen of brush he dragged it, thirty yards or better before stopping to rest. It felt lighter. He pulled it the rest of the way to the pit without stopping and then he couldn't breathe any more. He lay in the grass very quietly, waiting for the shoulder to stop, and held on to the leg, afraid if he turned loose he would not touch it again. His breath came back and he sat up a little, not hurting, conscious only of his hand hooked around the suppurant flesh. Then he got to his feet, jerked the body to the edge of the pit in three long steps, talking in a voice skirting hysteria: You son of a bitch. You rotten son of a bitch.

Dropping the leg he planted one foot in the man's side and shoved him violently over the rim, the arms flapping briefly in some simulation of protest before crashing into the moldery water below.

Going back down the mountain he left the ruts twice,

cutting a swath the second time through a stand of sumac one of which caught in the bumper and rode there like a guidon. A limb whipped in the window and laid open his cheek. He didn't even know the trunk was open until a car passed him on the pike where he had forced himself to slow down and he realized that he had seen no lights in the rearview mirror.

From his log the old man watched the shape of the retreating lights cutting among the trees. When they went from sight he brought a pipe from his jacket, filled and lit it. The dogs had treed some time past and their calls were now less urgent. He smoked his pipe down, knocked out the ashes on the log and rose stiffly, fingering a chambered goat-horn slung from his neck by a thong. Low in the east a red moon was coming up through the clouds, a crooked smile, shard of shellrim pendant from some dark gypsy ear. He raised his horn. His call went among the slopes echoing and re-echoing, stilling the nightbirds, rattling the frogs in the creek to silence, and on out over the valley where it faded thin and clear as a bell for one hovering breath before the night went clamorous with hounds howling in rondelays, pained wailings as of phantom dogs lamenting their own demise. From the head of the hollow Scout and Buster yapped sharply and started down the creek again. The old man lowered his horn and chuckled, turned down the gully wash taking the stickrimmed basins like stairs, cautiously, turning as alternate feet descended. He had cut a pole of hickory, hewed it octagonal and graced the upper half with hex-carvings—nosed moons, stars, fish of strange and pleistocene aspect. Struck in the rising light it shone new white as the face of an apple-half.

The Green Fly Inn burned on December twenty-first of 1936 and a good crowd gathered in spite of the cold and the late hour. Cabe made off with the cashbox and at the last minute authorized the fleeing patrons to carry what stock they could with them, so that with the warmth of the fire and the bottles and jars passing around, the affair took on a holiday aspect. Within minutes the back wall of the building fell completely away, spiraling off with a great rushing sound into the hollow. The rooftree collapsed then and the tin folded inward, the edges curling up away from the walls like foil. By now the entire building was swallowed in flames rocketing up into the night with locomotive sounds and sucking on the screaming updraft half-burned boards with tremendous velocity which fell spinning, tracing red ribbons brilliantly down the night to crash into the canyon or upon the road, dividing the onlookers into two bands, grouped north and south out of harm's way, their faces lacquered orange as jackolanterns in the ring of heat. Until the stilts gave and the facing slid backward from the road with a hiss, yawed in a slow curvet about the anchor of the pine trunk, overrode the crumpling poles, vaulting on them far out over the canyon before the floor buckled and the whole structure, roof, walls, folded neatly about some unguessed axis and dropped vertically into the pit.

There it continued to burn, generating such heat that the hoard of glass beneath it ran molten and fused in a single sheet, shaped in ripples and flutings, encysted with crisp and blackened rubble, murrhined with bottlecaps. It is there yet, the last remnant of that landmark, flowing down the sharp fold of the valley like some imponderable archeological phenomenon.

II

Curled in a low peach limb the old man watched the midmorning sun blinding on the squat metal tank that topped the mountain. He had found some peaches, although the orchard went to ruin twenty years before when the fruit had come so thick and no one to pick it that at night the overborne branches cracking sounded in the valley like distant storms raging. The old man remembered it that way, for he was a lover of storms.

The tank was on high legs and had a fence around it with red signs that he had been pondering for some time, not just today. From time to time he sliced a bite from one of his peaches. They were small and hard, but he had good teeth. He propped one foot up in the limb with him and fell to stropping the knife slowly on the smooth-worn toe of his boot. Then he wet a patch of hair on his arm and tested the blade. Satisfied, he reached for another peach and began peeling it.

When he had finished this one he wiped the blade of the knife on his cuff, folded and pocketed it, passed a handful of loose sleeve across his mouth. Then he got down from his limb and started up through the wreckage of the orchard, threading his way among the old gray limbs and stopping to look out over the valley now and again, at the black corded fields and the roofs winking in the sun. When he came out on the road he turned down to the right, his brogans making small padding sounds in the red dust, his huge knobby-kneed trousers rolling and moiling about him urgently as if invested with a will and purpose of their own.

This was the orchard road red and quiet in the early sun, winding from the mountain's spine with apple trees here along the road and shading it, gnarled and bitten trees, yet retaining still a kept look and no weeds growing where they grew. Farther up was a side road that went off among the trees, shade-dappled, grass fine as hair in the ruts. It went to the spray-pit, a concrete tank set in the ground that had once been used to mix insecticide. These six years past it had served as a crypt which the old man kept and guarded. Passing it now he remembered how he had been *coming up from the hollow with a gallon bucket when a boy and a girl, neither much more than waist-high to him, had rounded the curve. They stopped when they saw him and it took him a while, coming toward them with his pail, to see that they were scared, huge-eyed and winded with running. They looked ready to bolt so he smiled, said Howdy to them, that it was a pretty day. And them there in the road, balanced and poised for flight like two wild things, the little girl's legs brightly veined with brier scratches and both their mouths blue with berry stain. As he came past she began to whimper and the boy, holding her hand, jerked at her to be still, he standing very straight in his overall pants and striped jersey. They edged to the side of the road and turned, watching him go by.*

He started past, then half turned and said: You'ns find where the good berries is at?

The boy looked up at him just as though he hadn't been watching him all the time and said something which cracked in his voice and which the old man couldn't make out. The girl gave up and wailed openly. So he said:

Well now, what's wrong with little sister? You all right, honey? Did you'ns lose your berry bucket? He talked to them like that. After a while the boy began to blubber too a little and was telling him about back in the pit. For a few minutes he couldn't figure out what was the pit and then it came to him and he said:

Well, come on and show me. I reckon it ain't all this bad whatever it is. So they started up the road although it was pretty plain they didn't want to go, and when they turned down the road to the spray-pit the boy stopped, still holding the little girl's hand and not crying any more but just watching the man. He said he didn't want to go, but for him, the old man, to go on and see. So he told them to wait right there that it wasn't nothing.

He saw the berry pails first, one of them turned over and the blackberries spilled out in the grass. A few feet beyond was the concrete pit and even before he got to it he caught a trace of odor, sour . . . a little like bad milk. He stepped onto the cracked rim of the pit and looked down into the water, the furred green top of it quiet and touched with light. Sticks and brush poked up at one corner. The smell was stronger but other than that there was nothing. He walked along the edge of the pit. Down the slope among the apples some jays were screaming and flashing in the trees. The morning was well on and it was getting warm. He walked halfway round, watching his step along the narrow sandy concrete. Coming back he glanced down at the water again. The thing seemed to leap at him, the green face leering and coming up through the lucent rotting water with eyeless sockets and green fleshless grin, the hair dark and ebbing like seaweed.

He tottered for a moment on the brink of the pit and then staggered off with a low groan and locked his arms about a tree trying to fight down the coiling in his stomach. He didn't go back to look again. He got the berry pails and went back to the road, but the children weren't there and he couldn't think how to call them. After a while he called out, Hey! I got your berry buckets . . .

Some wind turned the apple leaves, shadow of a buzzard skated on the road and broke up in the fencing of briers. They were gone. He walked up the road a way, then back down, but there was no trace of them.

Three days later when he came back it was still there, no one had come. With his pocketknife he cut a small cedar tree with which to put it from sight.

It was still there, what of it had weathered the seasons and years. He went on along the road, an old man pedaling the scorched dust.

The sun was high now, all the green of the morning shot with sunlight, plankton awash in a sea of gold. Even late spring had dried nothing but the dust in the road, and the foliage that overhung either side had not yet assumed its summer coat of red talc. In the early quiet all sounds were clear and equidistant—a dog barking out in the valley, high thin whistle of a soaring hawk, a lizard scuttling dead leaves at the roadside. A sumac would

turn and dip in sudden wind with a faint whish, in
the woods a thrush, water-voiced . . .

The old man took a sidepath that led along a spur
of the mountain, cutting a spiderstick as he went to
clear the way where huge nets were strung tree to tree
across the path dew-laden and glinting like strands of
drawn glass, bringing them down with a sticky whisper
while the spiders fled over the wrecked and dangling
floss. He came out on a high bald knoll that looked
over the valley and he stopped here and studied it as a
man might cresting a hill and seeing a strange landscape
for the first time. Pines and cedars in a swath of dark
green piled down the mountain to the left and ceased
again where the road cut through. Beyond that a field
and a log hogpen, the shakes spilling down the broken
roof, looking like some diminutive settler's cabin in
ruins. Through the leaves of the hardwoods he could
see the zinc-colored roof of the church faintly coruscant
and a patch of boarded siding weathered the paper-gray
of a waspnest. And far in the distance the long purple
welts of the Great Smokies.

If I was a younger man, he told himself, I would move
to them mountains. I would find me a clearwater branch
and build me a log house with a fireplace. And my bees
would make black mountain honey. And I wouldn't care
for no man.

He started down the steep incline. —Then I wouldn't
be unneighborly neither, he added.

The path followed along the south face of the mountain and came out on the pike; a dirt road dropped off
into a steep hollow to the left. The old man went this
way, down under the wooded slope where water dripped
and it was cool. Half a mile farther and the road turned
up a hill, emerging from the woods to poke through a
cornfield where a brace of doves flushed out and faired

away to the creek on whistling wings. Beyond the field
and set back up from the road was a small board shack
with the laths curling out like hair awry, bleached to a
metal-gray. It was to this place that the man came, carrying the stick across his shoulders now as one might
carry a yoke of waterbuckets, his hands flapping idly.

The hillside in front of the house was littered with
all manner of cast-off things: barrel hoops, a broken
axehead, fragments of chicken-wire, a chipped crock . . .
small antiquated items impacted in the mud. There was a
black hog-kettle which he didn't use any more; it was
flecked with rust. The porch was shy the first step
and he had to climb up, using his stick for support. The
front of the house in the shade under the porch roof
was green with fungus and the old man sat wearily
on the floor and leaned back against it, stretched his legs
out flat and opened his collar. It was damp and cool.
The house faced to the north with a slope of trees
behind it and snow lay in his yard longer than in most
places.

In spring the mountain went violent green, billowing
low under the sky. It never came slowly. One morning
it would just suddenly be there and the air rank with the
smell of it. The old man sniffed the rich earth odors,
remembering other springs, other years. He wondered
vaguely how people remembered smells . . . Not like
something you see. He could still remember the odor of
muskrat castor and he hadn't smelled it for forty years.
He could even remember the first time he had smelled
that peculiar sweet odor; coming down Short Creek one
morning a lot more years ago than forty, the cottonwoods white and cold-looking and the creek smoking.
Early in the spring it was, toward the close of the trapping season, and he had caught an old bull rat with
orange fur, the size of a housecat. The air was thick with

the scent of musk and had reminded him then of something else, but he could never think what.

He dozed, slept, for a long time. Late in the afternoon clouds began to pile up in the gap of the mountain and a fresh breeze came past the corner of the porch to rock gently the gourds swung from the eaves.

He woke before the rain started. The breeze had cooled and cooled, fanning his face and the beads of sweat on his forehead. He sat up and rubbed his neck. A pair of mockingbirds were pinwheeling through the high limbs of the maples, were still; and then, arriving as if surprised themselves in the greengold heat of the afternoon, the first drops of rain splatted dark on the packed mud below the house. A flat shade undulated across the yard, the road, and climbed the mountain face with an illusion of sudden haste; the rain increased, growing in the distance with the wind and leaching the trees beyond the creek lime-silver. The old man watched the rain advance across the fields, the grass jerking under it, the stones in the road going black and then the mud in the yard. A gust of spray wet his cheek and he could hear the roof-shakes dancing.

When the one gutterpipe wired to the porch roof overflowed, the water fell in a single translucent fan and the landscape bleared and weaved. The rain splashed in until there was a dark border about the porch. He took out his tobacco and rolled a cigarette with trembly hands, neat and perfect. The wind had gone and he sat back with his head against the green plankings and watched the smoke standing in the air under the dampness and very blue. After a while the rain began to slacken and it was darkening, the sky above the mountain black but for a thin reef of failing gray, and then that was gone and it was night, staccato with lightning in the distance. The old man began to feel a chill and was ready to go in when something cracked on the mountain and he looked up in time to see the domed metal tank on the peak illuminated, quivering in a wild aureole of light. There was a sound like fingernails on slate and the old man shivered and blinked his eyes, the image burning white hot in the lenses for another moment, and when he looked again it was gone and he stood in darkness with the sound of the rain slipping through the trees and a thin trickle of water coming off the roof somewhere to spatter in a puddle below. He waggled his hand in front of his face and couldn't even see it.

He stood up and batted his eyes. Far back beyond the mountain a thin wire of lightning glowed briefly. Corner post and porch began to materialize slowly out of the murk and he could see the hound when it loomed up over the edge of the porch, snuffling, ears flapping and collar jingling as he shook the rain from his reeking hide. He came up, toenails clicking on the planks, and snuffed at the old man's trousers.

Where you been, old dog? the old man said. The dog began to rub against his leg and the old man pushed him away with his foot, saying Go on, Scout. Scout moved over against the house and settled. The man rubbed the back of his neck, stretched and went in.

The house was musty, dank and cellar-like. He felt his way to the corner table and lit a coal-oil lamp, the ratty furniture leaping out from the shadows in the yellow light. He went into the kitchen and lit the lamp there, took down a plate of beans and a pan of dry cornbread from the warmer over the stove. He sat at the table and ate them cold, and when he had finished went outside with a handful of biscuits and threw them to the dog. The rain had almost stopped. The hound bolted down

the biscuits and looked up after him. The screendoor
banged to, the square of light on the porch floor narrowed and went out with the click of the latch. The old
man did not appear again. The dog lowered his head on
his paws and peered out at the night with wrinkled and
sorrowing eyes.

Cats troubled the old man's dreams and he did not
sleep well any more. He feared their coming in the night
to suck his meager breath. Once he woke and found one
looking in the window at him, watching him as he slept.
For a while he had kept the shotgun loaded and lying on
the floor beside the bed but now he only lay there and
listened for them. Very often they would not start until
late and he would still be awake, his ears ringing slightly
from having listened so long. Then would come a thin
quavering yowl from some dark hollow on the mountain. He had used to trot to the window and peer out
at the hills, at the silhouette of pines in the low saddle
above Forked Creek like a mammoth cathedral gothically
spired . . . Now he only lay in his gray covers and listened. He did not sleep much at night and he was sore
and bone-worn from napping in chairs, against logs and
trees, sprawled on the porch.

When he was a boy in Tuckaleechee there was a col-
ored woman lived in a shack there who had been a slave.
She came there because, as she said, there weren't any
other niggers and because she felt the movements and
significations there. She wore a sack of hellebore at her
neck and once he had seen her on the road and hadn't
been afraid of her, as he was very young then, so she
put three drops of milfoil on the back of his tongue and
chanted over him so that he would have vision. She told
him that the night mountains were walked by wampus

cats with great burning eyes and which left no track even in snow, although you could hear them screaming plain enough of summer evenings.

Ain't no sign with wampus cats, she told him, but if you has the vision you can read where common folks ain't able.

He related this to his mother and she held the cross of Jesus against his forehead and prayed long and fervently.

The old man lay on his back listening to the heart surge under his ribcage, his breath wheening slow and even. In the fall before this past winter he had come awake one night and seen it for the second time, black in the paler square of the window, a white mark on its face like an inverted gull wing. And the window frame went all black and the room was filling up, the white mark looming and growing. He reached down and seized the shotgun by the barrel, spun it around and thumbed the hammer and let it fall. The room erupted . . . he remembered the orange spit of flame from the muzzle and the sharp smell of burnt powder, that his ears were singing and his arm hurt where the butt came back against it. He got up and stumbled to the table, dragging the gun by its warm barrel, found and struck a match and got the lantern lit. Then he went to the window, the light flickering thin shadows up the wall, playing to the low ceiling and whitening the spiderwebs. He held the lamp up. Above the window the boards were blasted and splintered clean and honeycolored. He didn't keep the shotgun by the bed any more but over in the corner behind the table.

The old man lay awake a long time. Once he thought he heard a cry, faintly, beyond the creek and the field, but he wasn't sure. A car passed on the road and he wondered about that but then he dozed and the crickets had already stopped.

Deep hole between her neck-cords, smokeblue. Laddered boneshapes under the paper skin like rows of welts descending into the bosom of her dress. Eyes lowered to her work, blink when she swallows like a toad's. Lids wrinkled like walnut hulls. Her grizzled hair gathered, tight, a helmet of zinc wire. Softly rocking, rocking. A looping drape of skirt slung in a curtain-fold down the side of the chair swept softly at the floor. She sat before the barren fireplace stitching buttonholes in a shirt of woolen millends. From out his scrolled and gilded frame Captain Kenneth Rattner, fleshly of face and rakish in an overseas cap abutting upon his right eyebrow, the double-barred insignia wreathed in light, soldier, father, ghost, eyed them.

With the lamps aligned one on either side she had a ritualistic look, a nun at beads perhaps. Later he watched from the kitchen lean-to because it had a tin roof and a wind had come up now and was blowing the rain across it with long ripping sounds like silk tearing. He turned the pages of his magazine but he had read it so much that he scarcely looked at the pages any more; mostly he watched how the lampflame quivered and the polished work that bound the stove, burnt to peacock colors of bronze and copper, violet-blue, changed patterns, ran to whorls and flamepoints. He waved his hand over the glass and the blue canisters above the stove bowed.

In the kitchen the man on the mantel couldn't watch him any more either. After a while he put down the magazine and turned around in the chair, sat with his elbows propped on the back and watched out the window for lightning. Thin cracks of it far back over Winkle Hollow like heat lightning. There was no thunder, only the rain and wind.

The boy thought he could remember his father. Or perhaps only his mother telling about him . . . He remembered a man, his father or just some other man he was no longer sure. His father didn't come back after they moved from Maryville. He remembered that, the moving.

It was a house of logs, hand-squared and chinked with clay, the heavy rafters in the loft pinned with wooden pegs. There had been a loom in the loft but it had since been burned piece by piece for kindling. It was a huge affair of rough-cut wood that under the dust had retained even then a yellow newness. The rafters still looked that way. In the summer wasps nested over the boards, using the auger-holes where dowels had shrunk in some old dry weather and fallen to the floor to emerge out into the hot loft and drone past his bed to the window where a corner of glass was gone and so out into the sunlight. There had been mud-dobber nests stacked up the wide planks too but his mother had raked them all down one day and aside from the wasps there were only the borers and woodworms, which he never saw but knew by the soft cones of wood-dust that gathered on the floor, the top log beneath the eaves, or trailed down upon the cobwebs, heavy yellow sheets of them opaque with dust and thick as muslin.

The house was tall and severe with few windows. Some supposed it to be the oldest house in the county. It was roofed with shakes and they seemed the only part of it not impervious to weather and time, for they were blackened and split, and now curling in their ruin they seemed victims of a long-ago fire which the house had somehow escaped altogether, for it was sound and the logs were finely checked and seasoned. They sagged and bellied and seemed supported only by the chimneys of clay and river rock at either end, but the house was strong and settled and no wind could bring a creak from it.

They paid no tax on it, for it did not exist in the county courthouse records, nor on the land, for they did not own it. They paid no rent on either house or land, as claimants to either or both properties were non-existent in deed as the house itself. They paid Oliver Henderson, who brought water to them three times a week on his milk route.

The well hidden in the weeds and johnson grass that burgeoned rankly in the yard had long shed its wall of rocks and they were piled in the dry bottom in layers between which rested in chance interment the bones of rabbits, possums, cats, and other various and luckless quadrupeds.

He didn't know that, but only guessed because he had found a young rabbit in the well one spring and was afraid to climb down after it. He brought green things

to it every day and dropped them in and then one day
he fluttered a handful of garden lettuce down the hole
and he remembered how some of the leaves fell across it
and it didn't move. He went away and he could see for
a long time the rabbit down in the bottom of the well
among the rocks with the lettuce over it.

She had finished now and put one lamp on the mantel
and was looking at it with the shirt in her hand held up
against her. She stood that way for a while and then she
turned and saw him watching her over his shoulder, each
of them touched with light and the space between them
through the narrow door dark. He couldn't see her eyes
and he made out that he was looking at something else
and finally turned back to the window and the rain.

Boy, she said.

Yesm.

You get to bed.

Yesm, he said again. He did not move.

Your bed ain't got wet, is it?

No mam.

It would be wet, always was when it rained even if it
didn't blow. It was musty and smelled good then and
cool enough for the blanket. This year, this summer, he
had moved to the porch off the kitchen, carrying his bed
down one Sunday evening while she was at church and
in it by the time she got back, breathing deeply when
she stopped at the door on her way in. Then he could
hear her at the dishes in the kitchen humming to herself,
and she never said anything about it except she made
him carry out the two boxes of bottles and cans he had
evicted from the corner. The lean-to porch was screened
in from waist-high up; after he was in bed a while
he could see even the acorns in the yard oaks. Some
nights a tall gaunt hound came and peered in the screendoor at him and he would speak to it, it standing there

high-shouldered and flat-looking, not moving, and then it would be gone and he could hear its feet padding off through the yard and the clink of its collar.

He pulled the bed out from the corner, turned back the spread and felt the pillow. Then he turned it over and took the blanket from under his arm and put it on the bed and got in. That was the last night of that summer. He fell asleep to the water and metal sounds of the rain runneling over the tin and sluicing through the gutterpipe, the rapid slash of it in a gust of wind and the fine mist spraying his face through the bellying screen. The oaks stirred restlessly, low admonitions, shhh . . .

In the morning the rain had stopped and there was a chill in the air and smoke. He smiled at that, for he was waiting and weathers and seasons were his timepiece now. There were still warm days but that didn't matter to him. Jays were in the blackoaks mornings and the grackles had come back, great flocks of them bending the trees, their feathers glinting dark metal colors and their calls harshly musical, like a rusty swing. Or they would be on the ground, the yard rolling blackly with them, and he would run out and pop his hands once and see them explode sunward, a flapping shrieking horde bearing leaves and debris into the air on the updraft of their wings.

The first weeks of September went and the weather held and no frost. The veins were coming up in his arms and he would press them and then raise his fist and feel the blood in the soft tubes.

He was pushing time now and he could feel it give. She canned the remainder of the garden in two days and was after him to get his bed back up to the loft before he took cold. It rained and the pond went blood-red and one afternoon he caught a bass from the willows in water not a foot deep and cleaned it and held the tiny heart in the palm of his hand, still beating.

His bed was still on the porch. These nights he could not bear to be in the house. He would go out after dinner and come back at bedtime—and then out again directly she was asleep, walking the dark roads, passing by the shacks and houses, the people illumined yellowly behind the windowlights in gestures mute and enigmatic . . .

One night cutting through a field he came upon two figures struggling in the grass, naked, white and frantic in the gloss of the quarter-moon as stranded fish. He went on. They did not see him. When he got to the road he began to run, his shoes slapping loud on the asphalt till they burned and stung, ran till his chest was seared. Below the forks of the road in Stiefel's yard was a great tulip poplar. He crawled up the kept-grass bank and folded in the shadows of the trunk like a malefactor gone to earth, his breath dragging coals through his lungs.

He sat there for a long time, watching the lights go out one by one over the valley. Sound of voices close and urgent on the acoustic night air, doors falling to, laughter . . . An encampment settling for rest, council fires put out . . . In caverns by torchlight a congress of fiends and warlocks rattling old dry bones in wistful hunger.

You goin to hunt him out. When you're old enough. Goin to find the man that took away your daddy. (Remember: fierce and already aging face downthrust into his, sweetsour smell . . .)

How can I? He had begun to cry.

Your daddy'd of knowed how. He was a Godfearin man if he never took much to church meetin . . . The Lord'll show you, boy. He will not forsake them what believe. Pray and the way will be made known to ye. He . . . You *swear* it, boy.

His arm was growing numb with pain . . . could feel her tremble through the clutched hand . . . I swear, he said.

You won't never forgit.

No.

Never long as you live.

Long as I live.

Yes, she said.

Long as I . . .

I won't forgit neither, she said, tightening once more on his arm for a moment, leaning her huge face at him. And, she hissed, he won't forgit neither.

I live . . .

He never forgot. From somewhere in the darkness came the sound of a banjo, tentative chords . . . a message . . . what news? Old loves reconsummated, sickness, a child's crying. Silence now in the houses. Repose. Even to those for whom no end of night could bring rest enough. And silence, the music fled in the seeping amber warmth of innumerable dreams laid to death upon the hearth, ghostly and still . . . The morning is yet to the nether end of the earth, and he is weary. Bowing the grass in like sadness the dew followed him home and sealed his door.

Still the weather held, and the rain. The days were gray and misty and in the night the trees dripped and spattered. The pond had been bottled and he watched them drifting about one morning while still-fishing from the limestone ledge at the upper end. Later a man came in a skiff poling through the fog and he saw him stop what bottles skittered and jerked and lift up the lines to take off the fish. The man saw him and nodded his head and he nodded back. The skiff circled at the upper end and returned down the pond, silent but for the thud of the pole on the stern-boards.

He was pushing hard now and the days were bending under and cold weather came. His cot was still on the porch and daily he checked the undoing of the yard trees, woke to a red world with the sun wedged huge and squat in the mountain gap and the maples incandesced. Couched in his musty blanket he sniffed to test the air. A limp breeze water-wrought and tempered with smoke came lisping through the screen with no news yet.

He waited. In the slow bleeding month of October he watched, looking torpid and heavylidded as a toad, his nerves coiled and tuned like a waiting cat's.

One evening coming from the store he saw her on the road and she smiled at him and said Hidy. He nodded and went on, heard them giggle behind him. He hadn't seen her since late in the summer.

He was crossing Saunders' field and bound for the creek, the homemade crokersack seine riding his shoulder like a tramp's dunnage. He never saw her until she spoke, leaning against a post with her hands capping the top of it and her chin resting on them. She looked as if she might have been standing there for days with an incalculable patience just waiting for him to come by.

Well, he thought, she ain't old enough to own the land to want to run me off of it even if she is big enough. So he said Howdy back to her.

Your name's John Wesley, ain't it?

He started to say, Yesm, but he said, Yep, that's my name.

She moved down from the post and came toward him, unhurried, sauntering. She wore a cotton print dress that

buttoned up like a housecoat and where it stretched
across her belly or strained to cover her rolling breasts
white flesh and pink silk pursed out between the buttons.
She pulled a weed and began chewing on it, eying him
sidewise, standing in front of him now and favoring one
leg so that her hip tilted out. What you doin? she asked.

Jest messin around, he said.

Messin around?

Yeah. That's all.

She nudged a stone with the toe of her slipper. Who
you messin around with?

Why, nobody. Jest me.

The tips of her breasts were printed in the cloth like
coins. She was watching him watch. You ain't supposed
to mess around with yourself, she told him, part of a
smile at her mouthcorners and eyes squinting in mischief.

Who says that? he asked.

Me. Preacher says that too.

I got to get on, he said.

You goin to mess with yourself some more?

He started on and she fell in alongside him. Where
you goin? she asked.

Pond, he said.

What you goin there for?

Fish.

Fish. Fishin? You ain't got a pole.

Got one over there, he told her. Hid.

You don't carry your pole with you?

Nah.

She giggled.

They were walking along slow, much slower than he
walked. After a while when she didn't say anything he
asked her where she was going.

Me? she said. I ain't goin nowhere. Jest messin around.

Who you goin to mess around with?

Hmph, she laughed. You'd like to know, wouldn't you?

Nah. I don't care who you mess with.

He walked on, looking up at the trees, the sky.

You carry your fish in that?

What's that?

She was pointing at the croker seine. That, she said.

Oh. Naw, that's a seine. I got to seine me some minners first afore I go to the pond.

She didn't leave. Wading up the creek poking the pole of the seine up under the banks he would see her walking along or standing and watching. Where the honeysuckles thinned at one place she came up to the bank and took off her shoes and kicked at the water with her toes as he went by. When he looked back she was in the creek to her knees with her skirt hiked up and tucked under in the waist of her bloomers and her thighs were incredibly white against the surge of brown water where she walked unsteadily into the current, leaning, her breasts swinging. She caught up to him and splashed water at him. She said:

You don't know my name, do you?

All right, he said. What's your name?

What do you care?

I don't care, you jest . . .

What'd you ast me for then?

You . . . I never . . . He stopped. You was the one ast me if . . .

Wanita, she said. If you jest got to know. Wanita Tipton. I live over yander. She motioned vaguely beyond the creek, across the late summer ruins of a cornfield, a stand of walnut trees surrounding a stained house with a green tin roof. He nodded, fell to seining again.

He didn't have enough floats and the minnows kept going over the back. Still he had half a dozen in the can tied to his belt.

You like to do this? she asked over his shoulder.

He turned around and looked at her. She was standing on a rock with her legs together. The back of her dress had come down and was dark and wet.

You got a leech, he said.

I got to what?

Leech, he said. You got one on your leg.

She looked down; it didn't take her long to find it, a fat brown one just below her knee with a thin ribbon of blood going pink on the wetness of her shin. She put her hand to her mouth and just stood there looking at it. It was a pretty good-sized leech for the creek although the pond leeches came much bigger. She just kept looking at it and after a while he said:

Ain't you goin to take him off?

That moved her. She looked up at him and her face went red. Goddamn you, she said. Goddamn you for a . . . a . . . Goddamn you anyway.

Hell, I never put him there.

Take it off! Damn you! God . . . will you take it off?

He sloshed over to where she was. Standing like that in water halfway to his waist and her up on the rock he could see up her thighs to where the skirt was tucked into her bloomers. He got hold of the leech, trying to look up and not to at the same time, and feeling giddy, shaky, and pulled it loose and flipped it past her onto the bank. He said: You ought not to wade barefooted.

He had felt for a minute that he wasn't even afraid of her any more and all he could remember now was running. *The huge expanse of flesh and the bloomers and her holding him by the collar with her feet somehow in the water on either side of him until he jerked away with his shirt ripping loudly and splashed back through the creek to the bank and out and across Saunders' field shedding water and minnows from his bucket with the foolish little seine still in his hand and water squishing in his shoes, running.*

She said something to the other one and they giggled again. He went on with his bread, home, his face burning in the chill of the low October sun. When he came in through the porch he saw that his bed was gone. She was in the kitchen. He put the bread on the table and went up to the loft, his tread hollow on the boxed steps, up to the cobwebby gloom under the slanting eaves where the bed had been set and made with fresh linen.

By now in the early mornings the pond was steeped in mist, thick and coldly swirling, out of which sounded the gabble of phantom ducks. At sunrise the whole valley would be glazed white and crystal and the air smoked and tangy from the stoves and later from the open fires where women gathered about the kettles with long wooden paddles, elvish-looking in their shawls and bonnets, a clutch of trolls at their potions. First days of frost, cold smoky days with hogs screaming and now and again the distant hound-calls of geese howling down the south in thin V's flattening on the horizon to a line and then gone. He cut wood, went out early to the rising stacks of new pine kindling rimed and shining in the morning frost like wedges of frozen honey. He worked hard at it and the days went. For that much time he would have buried the yard house-high in stovewood.

If he'd lived, she told him one evening, you wouldn't want for nothin. And him disabled in the war with that platmium plate in his head and all—turned down the govmint disability, he did. Too proud. Wouldn't take no handout from nobody even if it was the govmint. He was a provider all right, may the Lord God Jesus keep him.

Yes, she said, eying him doubtfully, you make half the man he was an you'll be goin some.

The fire ticked on in the little stove, cherrying softly the one side of it till the cracks in the old iron showed like thin spiders sprawled there.

Rocking quietly in her chair she had the appearance of one engaged in some grim and persevering endeavor in which hope was the only useful implement. Not even patience. As if perhaps in some indistinct future the chair itself would rise and bear her away to glory with her sitting fiercely sedate and her feet maybe tucked under the rung, her skirt gathered about her. She was humming something in her high nasal hum, faint evocation of summer bees. The coals chuckled, settled with easy sifting sounds. She rocked. That was how winter came that year.

Through the weary slide of the wiper on the glass, the water sluicing away, Sylder watched the rain dance in the lights, flash from the black road. Behind him the siren sounded again, louder and with a new sense of urgency. I never tried it in the rain, he was thinking. The accelerator pedal was crushed hard under his foot and he watched the needle strain upward to sixty before he let off for the next curve. Got to do it afore I start up the mountain, he told himself, or I'm in a sling. So it would have to be at the forks of the road.

Lightning glared in threatful illusions of proximity and quick shapes appeared in the road, leapt from ditch or tree in configurations antic and bizarre. Ghosts of mist rose sadly from the paving and broke in willowy shreds upon the hood, the windshield. One curve more.

Behind him the rear window blackened, then the slow
inexorable reach of lights crept out and fingered their
way across the hillside off to his left, remarking scrub
pines, ropes of limestone stretched in a yellow path like
rows of somnolent sheep. When he reached the top of
the hill the lights dropped away and the siren sounded
again.

I can take a wide sweep, he told himself hopefully.
The road looked like oil. Then there was no more time
and he was there, nerve and muscle on their own and
him just watching. He went into it at forty by the speedometer, saw the store blink its square eyes, cut the wheel
to the left, one hand locking for just a moment the
handbrake.

He couldn't see any more then. He brought the wheel
back, the brake already released. Except he couldn't pull
it sharp enough and the front end was sliding away and
not turning. Then it gave and a streaming herd of trees
swam past in the lights as if rushing headlong off the
very rim of the earth and the store loomed again, glazed
onto the green frieze, spinning past starkly white and in
incredible elongation. And yet once more, trees and
building in one long blur and then he was jarred from
the rear by a solid whump of a sound and heard something snap like a dry stick cracking and then a rattling
spray of glass. The lights had come to rest straight back
down the road and he already had the shiftlever up in
second, the tires whining, inching forward, when the
cruiser leapt over the hill before him. Then the tires bit
and he was gone, raking a fender of the other car on the
way out with deliberate skill. Behind him the store
squinted with half a post leaning in through one window
and a corner of the porch sagging down, abject and
humble in the pounding rain.

Sylder popped a match on the dash and lit a cigarette.

Adios, John, he said. He sang quietly to himself: Long
gone, ain't he lucky? Long gone, from Kentucky . . .
rocking slightly with the car's motion as it strung the
curves.

*I*t was in August that he had
found the sparrowhawk on the mountain road, crouched
in the dust with one small falcon wing fanned and limp,
eying him without malice or fear—something hard
there, implacable and ungiving. It followed his movements as he approached and then turned its head when
he reached out his hand to it, picked it up, feeling it
warm and palpitant in the palm of his hand, not watching
him, not moving, but only looking out over the valley
calmly with its cold-glinting accipitral eyes, its hackles
riffling in the wind. He carried it home and put it in a
box in the loft and fed it meat and grasshoppers for
three days and then it died.

Saturday he went into town with Mr Eller, holding
the bag in one hand and sitting up high in the cab of the
old truck watching the fields go by and then houses and

more of them and finally stores and filling stations, the river-bridge, and beyond that the shape of the city against the hot morning sky.

How you gettin back? Mr Eller asked.

I'll get back, he said. I got some things to do.

He was standing on the runningboard, one foot in the street at the corner of Gay and Main. Here, Mr Eller said, leaning across the seat, holding his hand down.

What?

Here.

I got money, he said. It's okay.

Go on, damn it, the man said. He was shaking the quarter at him. Behind them a horn sounded.

Okay, he said. He took the quarter. Thanks, I'll see ye.

He slammed the door and the truck pulled away, Mr Eller lifting his hand once in parting; he waved at the back of his head in the rear glass, crossed the street and went up the walk to the courthouse, up the marble stairs and inside.

There was a woman at a small desk just inside the door fanning herself with a sheaf of forms. He stood for a few minutes looking around the hall and reading the signs over the doors and finally she asked him what it was that he needed.

He held the bag up. Hawk bounty, he said.

Oh, she said. I think you go in yander.

Where's that?

Over there—she pointed to a hallway.

Much obliged, he said.

There was a long counter and behind it were other women at desks. He stood there for a while and then one of them got up and came over to him and said, Yes?

He hefted the ratty little bag to the counter. From the sweat-crinkled neck exuded an odor rich and putrid even above the stale musty smell of the old building. The

woman eyed the package with suspicion, then alarm, as
the seeping gases reached her nostrils. Delicately with
two fingers she touched the pinked mouthing of the
bag, withdrew. He upended it and slid the malodorous
contents out on the polished wood in a billowing well
of feathers. She stepped back and looked at it. Then she
said, not suspiciously or even inquiringly, but only by
way of establishing her capacity as official:

Is it a chickenhawk?

Yesm, he said. It's a youngern.

I see. She turned sharply and disappeared on a click
of heels behind a tier of green filing cabinets. In a few
minutes she was back with a little pad of printed forms,
stopping further down the counter and writing now
with a pen from a gathering of inkstands there. He
waited. When she had finished she tore the form from
the pad and came back and handed it to him. Sign where
the X's are, she told him. Then take it to the cashier's office. Down the hall—she pointed. He signed the two
lines with the pen, handed it back and started away when
she called him back.

I wonder if you would mind, she said, wrinkling her
nose and poking a squeamish finger at the little bird,
mind putting it back in the bag for me. He did. Holding
the slip of paper delicately in one hand and waving the
ink to dry he went to collect his bounty.

He left through the open door with the wind hollow-
ing through into the hall and skirmishing with the papers
on the bulletin board, warm wind of the summer fore-
noon fused with a scent of buckeyes, swirling chains of
soot about on the stone steps. He held the dollar in his
hand, folded neatly twice. When he got outside he took
it and folded it again, making a square of it, and thrust
it down between the copper rivets into the watchpocket
of his overall pants. He patted it flat and went down the

*walk past the grimy trees, the monuments, the poised
and interminably peering statue, and out to the street.*

*A band was playing, wavering on the heat of the city
strains of old hymns martial and distantly strident. Rows
of cars were herded in shimmering somnolence beneath
a vapor of exhaust fumes and at the intersection stood a
policeman at parade rest.*

*He crossed the street and the music came suddenly
louder as if a door had opened somewhere. When he got
to the corner he could see them coming, eight and ten
abreast, a solemn phalanx of worn maroon, the drill-
cloth seedy and polished even at that distance, and their
instruments glinting dully in the sun. In a little knot to
the fore marched the leader, tall-hatted and batoned,
and the four guidons bracing up their masts, the colors
furling listlessly. A pair of tubas in the mass behind
them bobbed and rode like balloons, leaped ludicrously
above the marchers' heads and belched their frog-notes
in off-counterpoint to the gasping rattle of the other
instruments. Behind the marchers came a slowly wend-
ing caravan of buses through the windows of which
flocks of pennants waved and fluttered.*

*He watched, gathered up and pressed in the crowd,
the people sweating in their thin summer clothes, a maze
of shapes and colors similar only in the dark patches
under their armpits, straining their necks, toe-standing,
holding up children. The marchers passed them under
the canopy of heat, sweaty and desperate-looking. He
saw the near tuba player redfaced and wild as if perhaps he were obliged to puff at his instrument to keep
it from deflating and drooping down over the heads of
his fellows. They passed in an enormous shudder of
sound and the buses came, laborious in low gear, churning out balls of hazy blue smoke, their windows alive
with streamers, pennants, placards, small faces. Long*

paper banners ran the length of the buses proclaiming for Christ in tall red letters, and for sobriety, offering to vote against the devil when and wherever he ran for office. One by one they passed and again the multicolored flags in small children's hands waving at the spectators who in turn mopped listlessly at their necks and faces with handkerchiefs. A blue and yellow card legended: Don't Make My Daddy a Drunkard fell to the street like a stricken bird, leaving an empty hand clutching at the window. The next bus splintered and ground the flagstem and printed tiretreads over the sign.

Then the music stopped abruptly and there was only the uneasy shifting of the crowd, the slow drone of the buses. The pennants and signs came gradually to rest, to a collective embarrassment as if someone had died and they went on that way until the last bus was by, the little faces looking out solemn as refugees, onto the bridge and so out of the city. The crowds ebbed into the streets and thinned and the traffic began, the cars moving and the streetcars clicking past.

He was still standing on the sidewalk and now he saw the city, steamed and weaving in heat, and rising above the new facings of glass and tile the bare outlandish buildings, towering columns of brick adorned with fantastic motley; arches, lintels, fluted and arabesque, flowered columns and crowstepped gables, baywindows over corbels carved in shapes of feet, heads of nameless animals, Pompeian figures . . . here and there, gargoyled and crocketed, wreathed dates commemorating the perpetration of the structure. Rows of pigeons dozed on the high ledges and the heat rose in visible waves up from the paving. He patted the folded dollar again and started up Gay Street. When he got to the Strand he stopped and studied the pictures advertising the Saturday serial and fingered the quarter. Then he turned left *and went up to Market Square. On the corner a man was screaming incoherently and brandishing a tattered Bible. Next him stood an old woman strapped into an accordion, mute and patient as a draft horse. He crossed the street behind the half-circle of spectators. The man stopped screaming and the accordion began and they sang, the two voices hoarse and high-pitched rising in a sad quaver to the calliope-like creaking of the instrument.*

He went up the far side of the square under the shadow of the market house past brown country faces peering from among their carts and trucks, perched on crates, old women with faces like dried fruit set deep in their hooded bonnets, shaggy, striated and hooktoothed as coconut carvings, shabby backlanders trafficking in the wares of the earth, higgling their goods from a long row of ancient vehicles backed obliquely against the curb and freighted with fruits and vegetables, eggs and berries, honey in jars and boxes of nuts, bundles of roots and herbs from sassafras to boneset, a bordello of potted plants and flowers. By shoe windows where shoddy footgear rose in dusty tiers and clothing stores in whose vestibules iron racks stood packed with used coats, past bins of socks and stockings, a meat market where hams and ribcages dangled like gibbeted miscreants and in the glass cases square porcelain trays piled with meat white-spotted and trichinella-ridden, chunks of liver the color of clay tottering up from moats of watery blood, a tray of brains, unidentifiable gobbets of flesh scattered here and there.

Among overalled men and blind men and amputees on roller carts or crutches, flour and feed bags piled on the walk and pencil pedlars holding out their tireless arms, past stalls and cribs and holes-in-the-wall vending tobacco in cut or plug, leaf or bag, and snuff, sweet or scotch, in little tins, pipes and lighters and an esotery of small items down to pornographic picture books. Past cafés reeking with burned coffee, an effluvium of frying meat, an indistinguishable medley of smells.

Under the Crystal's marquee of lightbulbs a group of country men stood gazing hard past the box office where a tired-looking woman sat beneath a sign: Adults 25— Children 11—watching the film through a missing panel of curtain. Sounds of hooves and gunfire issued onto the street. He couldn't see past or over them and went on by, up the square, until he stood before a window garnished with shapes of wood and metal among which he recognized only a few common handtools. He held his hand up to one eye to break the glare of light on the glass and he could see them in the dim interior, hanging from their nail on the wall. He checked the dollar and went in. His footfalls were muffled on the dark oiled floors, bearing him into an atmosphere heavy with smells of leather and iron, machine-oil, seed, beneath strange objects hung from hooks in the ceiling, past barrels of nails, to the counter. They were hanging down by their chains and looking fierce and ancient among the trace chains and harness, bucksaws and axehelves. A clerk passed behind the counter and waited on a man idly turning a brass doorknob in his hand. Together they disappeared into the gloom, ducking under a fringe of dangling strap leather, to the rear of the store. A few minutes later a grayhaired man came up the aisle and leaned on the counter looking down at him.

Can I hep ye, son? he said.

How much are they? He motioned vaguely past the man as if there were but one item of merchandise displayed there. The traps . . . your traps there.

The man turned. Traps? Steel traps.

Yessir.

Well, he said, let's see . . . what size?

Them. He pointed. Number ones.

The man studied the dull metal shapes as if aware for the first time of their existence, seemingly puzzled not over their price but as to how they came to be there in the first place. Then he said, Yes. And lifted one down and set it on the counter before the boy at a quarter-angle, straightening the chain, as one might show a watch or a piece of jewelry.

The boy touched the oiled smoothness of it, pan, trigger, jaws, spring. How much? he asked again.

Thirty cents.

Thirty cents, the boy repeated.

Lessen you buy by the dozen. They're three dollars the dozen.

The boy turned that over in his mind. That would make em twenty-five then, wouldn't it?

Well, the man said, twelve and three . . . four for a dollar . . . is right, twenty-five cents is right.

Well, he said, I aim to get a dozen but I cain't get all of em together at the same time. So I wonder if I couldn't get four of em today and then get the rest later on . . . ?

The man looked at him for a minute and then he smiled. Why I reckon you could, he said. Course you'd have to sign a pledge for the whole dozen so as for me to let you have the four at the dozen price.

The boy nodded.

He reached up and unhooked three more traps and put them on the counter, their chains rattling angrily, reached under the cash register and came up with a book of old order forms. He wrote in it for a while and then tore off two copies and handed one to the boy. Sign that, he said. He was holding out the pen.

The boy took it and started to write.
Better read it first, the man cautioned.
He read it, ciphering out the tall thin handwriting:

I, the undersigned, do hereby agree to purchase
8 (eight) Victor no. 1 traps from the Farm & Home
Supply Store prior to Jan. 1, 1941. Price to be @ 25
cents ea.

Signed. . . . .

signed his name to the bottom and handed back the pen.
The man took the signed paper and handed him the
other one, the carbon. Thisn's your copy, he told him.
The boy took it and folded it, then took the dollar from
his watchpocket and smoothed it on the counter. The
man took the dollar and rang it up in the register. Wait
till I get you a poke, he said.
He pulled a sheet of brown paper from a roll and
wrapped the traps in it and tied them with string. The
boy took the package, hefting the weight of it in his
hands. I'll be back to get the othern's afore long, he told
the man.
Then he was gone, out into the blinding sunshine
among the high-shouldered crowds, sped and well-
wished by an old man's smile.

They were still tied up in the brown paper and
wedged in back of the rafter. On the morning of the
fifteenth of November he got up early and crossed
the icy floor of the loft, reached in and pulled them
out and went back and sat in bed, feeling the shape of
them through the dusty paper. Then he undid the
string and dumped them out on the blanket. He set
them one by one and touched them off with his
thumb under the lower jaw and they leaped in his hand
and rang shut viciously. After a while he hung them
on a nail over the bed and went down to breakfast.

He was at the creek all that day wading in the steely water, poking among the dried honeysuckles, noting tracks and droppings, slides and dens. One sleeve was wet past the elbow where he had reached to feel an underwater hole and his toes were numb in the leaky kneeboots. By the time he got home he was chilled and shaking but he had his four sets laid.

When he left the house the next morning, quietly out through the lean-to, letting the door back softly, light was just coming low in the east, breaking along the gray ridges, and a cold rim of moon still hung over the mountain. The oaks were black and stark and the leaves in the yard were frosted and snapped under his feet with thin glassy sounds. He cut straight through the woods to Saunders' field, hoary and pale in the hazy cold of that first light, the dead grass sheathed in ice like slender bones, rock shoals lapped in mist and crows ambling stiff-legged on the far side where willows marked the creek's course. He crossed the fence, the icy wire in the web of his thumb like a cut. The crows skulked off on hooked wings to a clump of gray cedars. He quartered across the field, crossed another fence, near to the creek now, under the mountain, past the slain corn in hushed and battered flanks where doves had fed till late. Already he could hear the riffle and purl of the water and then he was out on the high bank where the slide went down —a slash of packed clay casehardened with frost and pressed with the scrabble-marks of muskrats—and below in the water his trap lying in wait still. He went on up the creek, crossed a shelf of limestone where periwinkles crowded and watercress swayed in the current. In a honeysuckle tunnel reeds and grasses were tramped down and a tangled sheaf of white weed stalks floated over his second trap. The other two were close together just below the pike bridge and there were no sleek muskrats in them either. The creek clattered down through green stone grottoes, over the rocks, curling, eddying under the white roots of cottonwoods where crawfish peered out with stemmed eyes. And the sun running red on the mountain, high killy and stoop of a kestrel hunting, morning spiders at their crewelwork. But no muskrats struggled in his sets.

After five mornings he pulled one trap and carried it to the bridge. There were fresh tracks on a siltbar there and he set his trap in the shallow water where they came and went. Two mornings later the trap was pulled out in the creek and there was a toenail clamped in the underside of the jaws. He reset it and was at the creek an hour before daylight in the morning with a flashlight.

Light pale as milk guided the old man's steps over the field to the creek and then to the mountain, stepping into the black wall of pineshadows and climbing up the lower slopes out into the hardwoods, bearded hickories trailing grapevines, oaks and crooked waterless cottonwoods, a quarter mile from the creek now, past the white chopped butt of a bee tree lately felled, past the little hooked Indian tree and passing silent and catlike up the mountain in the darkness under latticed leaves scudding against the sky in some small wind. Light saw him through the thick summer ivy and over windfalls and limestone. Past the sink where on a high bluff among trilobites and fishbones, shells of ossified crustaceans from an ancient sea, a great stone tusk jutted.

The old man kept to a steep path off to the right and

came through the last thick brush to the mountain road, breathing heavily. He stopped there to lean on his cane and the first slant light of moon topped the mountain on the far side so that the crest of it was washed in a watery silver and the dust of the road shone like mica. A half mile to his left was the circle at the end of the road and beyond that the fence and the installation. The road to the spray-pit was but a few yards to the right of where he stood in the road now, hearing his breath soar out in the silence. He looked as one peering from vast heights, the sky seeming to lie below him in a measureless spread, flickering like foil by half-light and gleaming lamely into shadow where it folded to the trees.

Years back on summer nights he used to walk with neighbor boys two miles to the store to buy candy and cigars. They would come back over the warm and deserted roads talking and smoking the cigars. One night taking a shortcut they passed a house and saw through one window a woman undressing for bed. The others had gone back for a second look but he would not go and they laughed at him. The old man remembered it now with dim regret, and remembered such nights when the air was warm as a breath and the moon no dead thing. He started down the road to the orchard path and to the pit for this second look.

The moon was higher now as he came past the stand of bullbriers into the orchard, the blackened limbs of the trees falling flatly as paper across the path and the red puddle of moon moving as he moved, sliding sodden and glob-like from limb to limb, fatly surreptitious, watching as he watched. His feet moved ahead of him, disembodied and unfamiliar, floating through the banded shadows, and the limecolored grass swished and folded, breaking to light-shivered undersides like glass splintering softly, catching the pale light and then rushing to darkness. Excepting the counterpoint of crickets there was no other sound.

Where the road curved to bring into view the clearing, the dim outline of the pit, the old man paused. The glade seemed invested with an aura of antiquity, overhung with a silence both spectral and reverent. He could feel something cold rising up in him and was almost of a mind to turn back. Taking a little tighter grip upon his cane he stood so for a while, then stepped into the clearing and came to the edge of the pit, ushering his own presence forward like a child to the pale gray lip of concrete stretched in the grass like a fallen monument, stepped up on it and looked into the black square of the pit incised geometrically into the earth.

The old man had visited here in the years past but never by night. Each winter he came and cut a cedar to serve for wreath and covering, the waxed and ciliate sprigs holding their green well into the spring before the heat blasted them and even then they held their shape, like reproductions in dull copper. It took a year's weather to fret them into the aromatic humus which steeped in what rainwater the pit held and so rendered in turn a tannic liquor dark as pitchblende by which the old man fancied had long been stained the wormscored bones that lay here. These things he observed, for he was a watcher of the seasons and their work. By the coming Christmas he would have cut the seventh cedar and with this he felt might come an end to his long deadwatch.

So he stood, looking down, and now he thought it less eerie than he had supposed, the half-darkness about him almost sheltering. Seeing that the range of his visibility extended at least partially into the pit he even sat down on the concrete edge and dangled his feet. He tugged a pipe from the folds of his overalls, filled it from a small sack of tobacco and lit it, puffing deeply, watched the smoke pale against the night by the matchflare. Then he held the match out over the pit and peered down, but he could not see even the rustcolored tips of the cedars and the match burned down to his thumb and he dropped it.

There was nothing. The dead had risen and gone; no revenant mourned here the unburied remains. Slanting down the near wall was a half square of light and he could see the blotches of moss and fungus on the pale concrete like land-shapes from some ancient atlas. But that was all. Then in the silence there came from the pit a single momentary water-sound, softly, a small, almost tentative slosh.

He got to his feet and stepped back, then turned and trotted back up the path with his queer shambling gait, neither a run nor a walk, waving his cane about curiously.

Back in the road he slowed his steps; his breath was rasping and his chest tight.

He wandered up the road a way and came to a cleared place where he could see down through the thin trees faced with light the slope of the ground pouring over like a waterfall to break somewhere below, and the small yellow pinholes, lights from shacks and houses, warmth and life, burning steadfast among the fitful lightning bugs. A dog barked. He squatted on one heel in the road, tilted his cane against his shoulder, laved a handful of the warm dust through his fingers. A light breeze was coming up from the valley.

To his right, off beyond the last black swatch of trees in silhouette cresting the nob, he could hear a long cry of tires on the curves; in a little while the sound of a motor racking the night. The car came through the cut of the mountain, howling brokenly in the windgap.

Fine pencils of light appeared far below him, swinging an arc, shadows racing on the lit trees and then lining down the road and the car hurtling into sight, small and black, pushing the lights ahead of it. It rocketed down the grade and in a thin and slowly fading wail of rubber slid to darkness again where the road curved at the foot of the mountain.

The old man's legs began to cramp under him and he rose and stood about trying to work the stiffness out of them. He balanced on one leg and bent himself up and down by the strength of his knee. Then he stooped all the way down and tried to raise himself, an old man, exercising at midnight on a mountain top—too old to get up that way, and that was the good leg too. He hadn't been able to do it with the other leg for years and it creaked like dry harness. It still had birdshot in it, above the knee and higher, almost (he could remember yet the doctor pointing to the last little blue hole) to where a man surely oughtn't to be hit. Years later the leg had begun to weaken. The head too, the old man told himself, and got up, looked out over the valley once more before starting up the road.

Toward Red Branch a dog barked again. Another answered, and another, their calls and yaps spreading across the valley until the last sound was thin and distant as an echo. No dogs howled in the Hopper or down along Forked Creek where the old man lived. He thought of Scout bedded under the house, old and lame with his tattered hide half naked of hair, the bald patches crusted and scaly-skinned as a lizard. Scout with his hand-stitched belly and ribboned ears, split their length in places, whose brows so folded over his eyes that he could see at all only by holding up his head—which gave him an inquisitive air as he walked, as if he followed forever some wonderful odor strung out before him.

Big even for a redbone, a strong dog in his day, but he was seventeen years old. The old man had traded a broken shotgun for him when he was a pup.

He walked and ruminated and furrowed the dust absently with his cane until he came to the circle at the end of the road and the knoll beyond where the trees had been plucked from the ground and not even a weed grew. A barren spot, bright in the moonwash, mercurial and luminescent as a sea, the pits from which the trees had been wrenched dark on the naked bulb of the mountain as moon craters. And on the very promontory of this lunar scene the tank like a great silver ikon, fat and bald and sinister. When he got to the fence he stopped and leaned his cane and hooked his fingers through the mesh of the wire. Within the enclosure there was no movement. The great dome stood complacent, huge, seeming older than the very dirt, the rocks, as if it had spawned them of itself and stood surveying the work, clean and coldly gleaming and capable of infinite contempt.

He clung there wrapped in the fence for some time, perhaps the better part of an hour. He did not move except that from time to time he licked the cold metal of the diamonded wire with his tongue.

When the old man reached home again the moon was down. He did not remember coming back down the mountain. But there was the house looming, taking shape as he approached, and he felt that he had come a great distance, a sleepwalker who might have spanned vast and dangerous terrains unwittingly and unharmed.

As he turned his steps up the path a shadow swirled past his knees and fled soundlessly into the night.

In one corner of the front room there was an old wooden footlocker and the old man cleared away papers and clothes from the top of it and set the lamp on the floor close by. Then he undid the broken hasp and lifted it open. He rummaged through it, stopping now and again to examine some object: a brass watch weighing perhaps a quarter of a pound, a pair of cock-gaffs, a .32 rimfire revolver with owlhead grips and the hand broken so that the cylinder spun smooth as a barrel in water. Reams and sheafs of old catalogs and lists he thumbed through. An eight-gauge shotgun shell. At length he came up with a small square box decorated with flying ducks and this he set on the floor beside the lamp. He dropped the lid of the locker closed and the lamp flickered, on the wall a black ghoul hulking over a bier wavered.

He took the lamp and the box to the kitchen and placed them on the table. From the drawer he took a short curved meat knife and tested the edge on his thumb, pulled the drawer out further and reaching back in it came out with a worn gray piece of soapstone. With this he honed the knife, trying it from time to time on the hair of his arm until he was satisfied, then replaced the stone and opened the box. There were twelve bright red waxed tubes in it and he set them out on the table one by one, their dull brass bases orange in the lampglow. He selected one and with the knife made a thin cut around the base of the paper where the brass met. He examined it carefully, then deepened the cut, turning the shell against the blade. He checked it again, nodded to his nodding shadow and put the shell back in the box. He performed the same operation on the remaining eleven, putting each in turn in the box again. When he had finished he replaced the knife in the drawer and returned to the front room where he took them one by one, the twelve circumcised shotgun shells, and deposited them in the pocket of his coat.

Ef Hobie's father had been dead
too long for the people who admired Ef to remember
him. They were a whiskey-making family before whiskey-making was illegal, their family history mythical,
preliterate and legendary. They had neither increased
nor prospered and now Garland was the last surviving
son. Ef had died in a car wreck in 1937, less than a year
after coming out of Brushy Mountain. Not in the wreck
either—he lived three weeks and was even back on his
feet, where he wasn't supposed to be at all, and in the
store where people looked uneasily at his gaunt frame,
who had weighed just short of three hundred pounds.
He had been thrown clear of the car and then the car
had rolled on top of him and they had removed a good
part of his insides in the process of restoring him to
health. He was showing them the slick red scar that

angled across his withered paunch and sucking long drafts from an orange dope.

They performed a autopsy on me and I lived, he told them. Then he laughed and got down off the drink box, emptied his orange and reached to put it in the rack. The bottle clattered on the floor, he lurched once, wildly, collapsed into the bread rack and went to the floor in a cascade of cupcakes and moonpies.

So there were only two Hobies, Garland and his mother, and hard luck dogged them. Within the month Jack the Runner was arrested and sent up to Brushy for three years himself and county deputies broke into their smokehouse and took off what whiskey was there and took Mrs Hobie, aged seventy-eight, off to jail, sending her back home only when it was discovered she had cancer of the duodenum.

So Garland had to carry the whiskey up the mountain now to a den in the honeysuckles just below the circle and leave it there for Marion Sylder to pick up and haul to Knoxville. There was a gate across the orchard road since the installation had been set up on the mountain and only official carriers were permitted access —olive-painted trucks with gold emblems on the doors, passing in and out of the gate, the men in drab fatigues locking and unlocking the chain sedulously. With like diligence Sylder bolted and unbolted the ring-plate that held the chain on his comings and goings in the old Plymouth. But the two parties using the road kept different hours and they never met.

It was four o'clock in the morning when Sylder heard the old man shoot the first hole in the tank. He almost let go the case of whiskey he was carrying and then when the second shot came, hard upon the first, he set the case down carefully and stood dead still, waiting for cries, commands—an explanation. All was quiet. The birds were stilled in their first tentative and querulous chirpings. Low in the east and beyond the town a gray soulless dawn gnawed the horizon into shape. He was braced for another report, holding his breath, echoing the outrageously loud concussion in his inner ear before it came—two more shots, evenly spaced, something deliberate about them. Sylder made his way stealthily along the edge of the honeysuckle jungle, crossed an open space, arm of the orchard, going in the direction of the shooting.

When he got to the edge of the clearing where the installation stood he could see the man with the muzzle of the gun sticking through the fence-wire. He fired and the barrel came up short, sending waves out along the woven mesh and back. The man jerked under the recoil and the smoke spurted, slowed and billowed in the damp air. There were six neat black holes in the polished skin of the tank, angled up across it in a staggered line. The man broke the gun and picked the shells out. Slyder saw him hold them up for brief inspection before throwing them to one side, and saw them dance in the new light and knew what they were: the brass bases of the shells only, flicking and turning like coins as they fell.

The man was putting two more shells into the breech of the shotgun and Sylder could see them now, and the dull red of the waxed cardboard tubes that had been missing from the extracted cases. The man didn't hesitate; he raised the gun and breeched it in one quick motion. Two more blasts ripped the silence and two holes appeared now in the lower corner. He was making a huge crude X across the face of the tank. Again he examined the bits of brass before reloading.

Sylder watched wide-eyed from his retreat in the bushes. He could hear the solid whop of the full cases lamming into the tank and the tank seemed to reel under the impact like a thing alive. There was something ghastly and horrific about it and he had the impression that this gnomic old man had brought with him an inexhaustible supply of shells and would cease his cannonading only when he became too weary to lift the gun. He backed out of his hiding place and returned to the car. Daylight was coming on fast and he began to worry lest the old man's shooting bring investigation. He was late anyway and didn't know but that the legal, the official, carriers might use the road at this hour even if a crazy old man wasn't shooting holes in their responsibility with a shotgun and rung shells. There were six cases of whiskey still in the honeysuckles and he brought them out two at a time with a hobbling half-run. The firing had ceased. He got the turtledeck loaded and fastened, got in and started the motor. When he pulled out of the weeds and into the road he looked back and there was the old man standing on the hill above him at the turnaround, holding the shotgun in one hand and leaning on a cane. Sylder lowered his head and floorboarded the gas pedal.

When he was safe around the first curve he relaxed and drove slowly to the gate so as to leave as few signs as possible. He refastened the ring-plate and chain, got back in and turned onto the pike and toward Knoxville. Just beyond the creek he passed an olivecolored truck, the driver and the other man in the cab looking serious and official, but somewhat sleepy and not in any particular hurry. Genial, unofficial, and awake, Marion Sylder drove to town.

His light played on the wet mudbanks among roots and stumps, a sheaf of brown honeysuckle hanging down and trailing in the water like hair. His boots made suck-ing sounds as he waded against the slight current, walked softly the silted floor of the creek. He could hear a car on top of the mountain coming down, the exhaust rat-tling and the tires sounding on the switchbacks. He came to the bridge and waded to the spit of loam filled in against the concrete wall. Throwing his light to the set he could see the trap with the jaws cocked and the pan, all brown-looking under the water and wrinkling in the small ebb and lap of it. He put the flashlight in his pocket and squatted on the sand among tracks of feet and tails, wiggling his numb toes, huddling down in his mackinaw and breathing slowly into his cupped hands, listening in the darkness to the water curling past his feet with small muted water-sounds, to his cough echoing hollow and blankly among the beams overhead.

The tires sounded again, closer, and then the motor revving between engagements of the clutch and the explosive sound of the shift to high gear as the car came out of the last turn at the base of the mountain. He fol-lowed with his muscles the downward thrust of the lever, locked the shift home arm and shoulder. The car was on the straight stretch approaching the creek and he could feel the vibrations of it, waiting for it to pass over-head. It did not. He heard the motor building speed and then there was a sudden explosion, a doglike yelp, fol-lowed by a suspension of all sound, a momentary eclipse of animation even to the water and his own breathing.

The trees at his left leaped, wild with light, went out again. There came an eruption of limbs cracking, split-ting, of wrenched metal screaming like slate, a heavy and final concussion like a steel drum bursting. Silence again through which filtered a thin and diminishing rain of glass. By the pulsing wash of water at his feet he knew that it was in the creek and he tugged his flashlight free and poked the beam out along the bridge, the bank of the creek where broken saplings and peeled trunks stood out whitely all about like markers and finally to the sleek black flank of the car, upturned in the creek with the hood tilted into the water and the off-wheel still spinning idly. The side window-glass was laced with myriad cracks, shining in the beam like dewed spiderwebbing, and he could not see inside. The waterline angled across it, from cowl to centerpost, giving it an inverted look of anger.

By then he was already in the creek again, scrambling low under the beamed flooring of the bridge and dipping water into his boots with gentle sluicing sounds where he floundered in over the tops, squatting down too far under the canopy of sumacs broken over the bank, and the water on his backside icy as alcohol. He was thinking: I'll have to pull *up* on the doorhandle. Then he was at the car, stepping and threading the brush it had pulled into the creek with it, reached for the doorhandle, crammed it upward, and jerked back on it with his full weight.

It catapulted outward as if something inside had been galvanized into violent effort. shot open and pitched him backward through a tangle of down saplings and into the creek. In the darkness the water closed over him thickly as running oil, choking off his breath, filling his nose. He floundered to his feet streaming and numb, coughing up creek water. Wiping water from his eyes he looked about and saw the flashlight, still lit, scuttling downstream over the bed of the creek like some incandescent water-creature bent on escape. He waded after it, tearing recklessly about in the freezing water with the boots leaden and rolling about his shins, reached for it, his hand like a bat's shadow poised over the dome of light, and then it was gone, sucked down through the silt and mire inexplicably, and he was left balancing on one foot in the darkness with his arm and shoulder deep in the water. He groped about and finally came up with the flashlight and shook it. The metal cylinder sloshed softly water among the batteries. He stuck it in his pocket and surged noisily back upstream to the car.

He was aware for the first time now of a sickly-sweet odor, faintly putrescent, and by the time he reached the car again it was thick in the air and he knew it was whiskey without having ever smelled it. Then he could see the man taking shape out of the gloom, sprawled on the upturned headliner and half out through the open door, one arm hanging into the water. The sour smell of the whiskey, the mustiness of the old car upholstery, and what he perceived to be blood on the man's face— these burned such an image of death into his brain that he made for the bank, panicky, clawing wildly at the brush, up to the field where light in fragile shellpink reefs broke on an unreal world.

But the man wasn't dead. The boy was already on the bank, catching his breath and teetering with the dry rollings of his breakfastless stomach, when he heard a voice out of the void, hollow and half lost among the chatterings of the creek.

Hey, the call came.

He turned, hanging to a jagged sapling, saw in the shade below him a movement among the wreckage, a pale face against the dark interior of the car, the man propped up on his hands looking at him. Hey you, he said.

He hung there looking at him. A sweep of lights tracked the shadows of the mountain and a car hammered the bridge, echoing the noise of its passage in the creek. Finally he said: What do you want?

The man groaned. There was a moment of silence

and then he said, Goddamn, man; how about giving me a hand.

Okay, he said. He wasn't afraid any more, just cold, sliding down the mud and into the creek again and then squatting in the water facing the man, wondering what he should say. He could see him quite clearly now, there was a dark smear of blood down the side of his face. The man looked at him, a suggestion of a grin breaking painfully on his face. Played hell, didn't I? he said.

You hurt? His own words rattled like bb's through a clatter of teeth. He started to say something else but a further chill rendered him inarticulate, his palsied jaw jerking like an idiot's.

I don't rightly know, the man was saying. Yes. Here . . . he reached out one hand and the boy steadied it on his shoulder while the man drew up one knee and stepped out into the water. Then he pulled the other leg out, his face wrinkling with pain, and so was standing in the creek, his hand still on the boy's shoulder in an attitude of fatherly counsel. When he started for the bank the hand withdrew for a moment, one faltering half-step, and then flew back and clamped there like a predatory bird striking. Whew, the man said. I must of busted the shit out of my leg.

It took them some time to get up the bank, the boy trying to push him up and him pulling himself along by trees, roots, handfuls of dead grass, holding the leg out behind him. Then they sat in the weeds at the edge of the field breathing white plumes into the cold morning air. In the quarter-darkness the fields looked like water, flat and gray. The boy was wet and cold; everything was wet and very cold. The man ran his hand along his leg trying to tell whether it was broken or not. His trousers were clammy against his skin. The boy sat in front

of him hugging his shoulders and shivering, his toes lifeless, squishing in his boots when he wiggled them and
sand and grit rasping in his socks. He said: Your head's
bleeding.

The man ran his hand along the side of his face.

Other side.

He reached across and his hand came away sticky
with blood and he wiped it on his trouser leg and turned
to the boy. You want to do something for me?

Sure, the boy said.

Go down and get them keys then, and let's get the
hell out of here.

The boy disappeared over the cut of the bank; the
man could hear him in the water. Presently he came back
and handed the keys over.

Thanks, he said. Here. He took the boy's hand and
turned it over. What'd you do here?

The boy looked down at his palm. There was a black
and jagged line across it.

You jest do that? the man asked.

The boy looked at it dumbly. No, he said. I don't
think so. I must of done it when I fell in the creek.
Before . . .

The man dropped the keys in his pocket and struggled
to his feet. Well, come on, he said. We better get our-
selves patched up. This way, he added, seeing the boy
start for the road. He motioned toward the field and
set off with a hopping gait, muttering under his breath
Whew, Mother.

The boy followed him for a few paces, then quartered
off to the creek again and the man watched him go, his
legs disappearing in the mist, then the rest of him, so
that he seemed to be gliding away toward the line of
willows marking its course like some nightwraith fleeing

the slow reaching dawn until the man wasn't sure that he had really been there at all. Then he came back with a pole and handed it to him.

Thanks, the man said.

They moved on across the field, through vapors of fog and wisps of light, to the east, looking like the last survivors of Armageddon.

Their path led them up the creek, along the edges of the fields that terminated there—a curve of fields and the creek and the cupped slope of the mountain rising up to their right along which shafts of light now appeared laterally among the ghostgray trees. They struggled through the last fence, the boy holding the wire and trying to help him and him cussing, crossed a plank bridge at the fork of the creek, out through a cattle gate and onto the road, Henderson Valley Road.

The boy fastened the gate behind them and the man said, We got to stay off this road. They might of found it by now what with the light and all.

They crossed the road and started up a steep dirt drive on the other side. We can call here, the man said. The boy could see him better now. He needed a shave and the blood crusted on the side of his face was broken in fine cracks like old dark pottery where he winced with the pain of his slow progress, leaning heavily on the pole and breathing hoarsely. He was leanhipped and tall and his poplin jacket hung loosely about his shoulders. The boy thought he must be awfully cold dressed no warmer than that and wet to the knees besides. His own feet he couldn't feel at all now; they were like hooves rattling inside his boots. He hadn't stopped shivering the whole time. The drive climbed and turned and then there was a house.

It was an older man came to the door, a tremendous paunch slung in a gray and ragged undershirt drooped pendulously over the waist of his trousers like a sacked hog carcass. Out of a meaty face, jowled and white-stubbled with beard, two porcine eyes regarded them, blinking. Hot-toe-mitty, he said, slow and evenly. Then: Well, come on in if you're able. They entered, the man hobbling in with his pole and the boy following. The room was warm and suffused with odors of cooking meat.

Hey, old woman, their host called out, they's two fellers here jest fell out of a aryplane.

A woman came to the door at the far end and looked at them. Lord God, she said. She looked as if she might be going to say something else, then she clamped her jaw shut and disappeared with an air of briskness.

The room itself was comfortable with the new catalog store prosperity of china lamps, linoleum floors, a Warm Morning heater in front of which he installed himself while the two men stood talking. They paid little attention to him and he just watched them, the injured man waving his arms, telling the story, the other scratching alternately belly and head and saying Godamighty softly to himself from time to time by way of comment. After a while the woman came to the door again and called them in for coffee.

As they started for the kitchen the younger man motioned at him. This here is . . . he nodded to the boy.

John Wesley, he said.

John Wesley. This here is June Tipton—and this is his Mrs.

Mrs Tipton nodded back at him as they entered the kitchen and said, How do, John Wesley.

They sat down at the table and June said to the woman: John Wesley's the one what pulled Marion out of the creek.

She looked at her husband and then to him and smiled

appreciatively. The one called Marion was fishing through his pockets for cigarettes. That's right, he said. I might near of drownded.

She smiled again. After a while she turned to her husband and said, What all was he doin in the creek?

Jest laying there, June said. He blowed a tire and his car fell in.

She looked at the boy again and smiled and went on sipping her coffee demurely. The boy lowered his face to the steaming mug before him. Small waterdrops tripped down from his thawing hair, beaded and dropped from his earlobes. He was still in his soaked mackinaw and a puddle of water was gathering on the linoleum beneath his chair. Raising his eyes above the rim of the cup he saw the woman looking at him, leaning forward. She reached out and squeezed his coat. It made a funny squishing sound.

Lord God, she said, this youngern's wet clear through. He's a-fixin to take pneumony. She set down her cup and began pulling at the coat, trying to help him off with it. He seemed bent and tottering under the sheer weight of it.

They got him out of his coat and by then the man had finished his coffee and stood and he said he was ready to go if June didn't mind taking them.

So they thanked the woman, declining breakfast two or three times, and filed through the door, him holding the mackinaw in his arms now like a great bundle of wet wash, and got into a pickup truck parked behind the house and pointing down the drive. June kicked the blocks from under the front wheels and got in and they began rolling silently, gaining speed, and then he let in the clutch and the motor came to life angrily and they catapulted down to the road, turned left toward the mountain, the truck coughing and lurching and a bluish haze boiling up in the cab. He sat in the middle between the two men, trying to keep his knees clear of the gearshift. Through a missing slat in the floorboard he could see the gray road sliding under and a slip of bitter wind angled up one jean-leg.

They drove a mile or so up the mountain and turned into another drive not unlike the one from which they started. June turned the truck around in the yard and stopped and Marion opened the door and climbed painfully down. The boy waited.

Better come on in, Marion said. The boy turned and started to say something and then June said, behind him:

Reckon I better get on back.

Well, he said, I sure am much obliged. John Wesley, you better come on in and get dried out some; your old lady'll skin you for shoe leather.

So he clambered out of the truck and slammed the door, the truck already moving and June waving at them, and he and the man started for the house. It was full light now, the air smoky and cold. A woman was standing in the door with her arms crossed, holding her shoulders. She let them past and came in, closing the door behind her.

Mornin, the man said cheerfully.

Are you hurt? she asked. She was small and blond and very angry-looking.

Breakfast ready? he wanted to know.

She looked like she might be going to cry, her face crumpled a little and her chin quivering. Damn you, she said. Won't nothin do till you've killed yourself, is they? Why you ain't dead afore now is a mystery to me and God too I reckon, as I don't see why He'd have any call to look out after the likes of you any more than . . . she broke off suddenly and looked at the boy, standing there holding the coat in his arms and still dripping water. What about him, she pointed. Your helper. He hurt?

The boy looked down at himself, soggy and mud-splattered, seeds and burrs collected on his waterdark jeans like some rare botanical garden being cultivated there, at his rubber kneeboots with twigs and weeds sticking out of them, feeling the blisters they'd worn and the cords in his ankles pulled from walking in them. One sock was completely off and scrunched down some-where in the toe of the boot. I ain't no helper, he said. I jest found him.

He shot a glance up at the man. He was grinning. Don't let him fool you, he said. He was drivin. But he ain't hurt I don't reckon. I ain't neither, my leg is jest wore out fightin that dashboard.

Your head's wore out is what's wore out, she said. You get out of them clothes. Here, set down. She guided him to a sofa and began trying to undo the laces of his shoes.

The boy stood about uneasily, wondering what he was supposed to do. She got the man's shoes off and his socks. Now she was unfastening his belt. He just sat there, quiet and unresisting, as if engaged in some deep speculation. She kept saying Damn you, damn you, in a tone of despair and solicitude at once.

She was pulling his trousers off. The boy began to look about him wildly.

What are you doin? the man said in mock indignity. You raise up, damn you!

Here! he said. I'm in no shape for this kind of carry-in-on.

Marion Sylder, I'm not puttin up with your foolish-ness, you hear me? Now you get out of them britches and get out of them now and quick. God rest your poor mother I don't know why she ain't dead either puttin up with you long as she did . . . lift your feet. You . . . here, wait. I'll get you some shoes too. She disappeared through a door and the man winked hugely at him, sitting there with his trousers in a pile under his feet.

She came back and dumped some clothes into his lap —then she saw the great bruise on the side of his calf, livid in hues of red and purple against the bare white of his naked legs. She knelt and touched it, whimpering softly. She went out again and returned with a basin of water and a cloth and bathed it carefully, the man crying out from time to time in simulated anguish. But she didn't cuss him any more. When she finished she turned to the boy. What about you? she said.

Yesm?

Yesm? She looked from him to the man and back. You goin to die standin there I reckon, Yesm. She narrowed her eyes at him. Start shuckin, she said.

What?

The man on the couch giggled. He was pulling on a clean shirt.

Here, she said, go in yonder. She pointed behind her. I'll get you some clothes in jest a minute.

He started past her with strange sluicing sounds.

Empty them boots first, she told him.

He stopped.

Outside.

He said Yesm again, went to the door and returned, one sock on and one off, leaving odd unmatched tracks on the raw pine flooring.

The door she pointed him through led to a bedroom. There was a fireplace with a coal grate and a faint warmth still issuing from it. He stood in front of it on a small hooked rug for a minute, then softly eased the door to.

Get that blanket, the woman called to him.

He peeled off his wet clothes, piling them on top of the mackinaw which he had laid carefully on the floor, took the rolled blanket from the foot of the bed and wrapped himself in it.

He was standing at the window looking out at the gray morning when she came in with the shirt and pants and handed them to him. Then she scooped his things off the floor and went out. He unfolded himself out of the blanket and got into the dry clothes. There was a pair of army socks too and he put these on and sat on the bed, wondering if it was all right to walk on the floor with them. She didn't bring any shoes though and after a while he ventured out into the front room again. The man was dressed, his head bandaged, and he was sitting with his feet in a pan of water and reading a magazine. He looked up and saw the boy standing there in the drooping shirt and the trousers turned up at the bottoms and gathered at the waist by the expedient of fastening the front buttonhole to a suspender button on the side.

They ain't much of a fit, are they? the man said.

Nosir.

Marion.

What?

Marion. Sylder. That's my name, Marion Sylder.

Oh, he said.

Pleased to meet ye.

Yessir.

Well, the man said, get ye a chair.

He pulled up a cane rocker from beside the stove, sat quietly with his hands on his knees. The man leaned back on the sofa, a huge shapeless affair draped with a flower-print cover. Behind him on the wall in an oval frame hung a picture of him and the woman, the wife, peering out upon the room with tentative and uncertain smiles. There were small rugs scattered about the floor, some pieces of furniture—a sideboard, a table and chairs. On a small cabinet in one corner stood a walnut trophy with a small bronze automobile perched on top of it.

You know what was in the car?

The boy looked back at him. Yessir . . . Marion.

Well, the man said. He returned to his magazine, leafed a page over slowly, looked back at the boy. He grinned. It was good stuff too, he said. Sixty gallons of it.

Then the woman called them to breakfast and he put down the magazine and reached for a towel to dry his feet with. The boy noticed that part of the big toe was missing from the man's left foot. It was nailless, curious-looking, sort of like a nose. The man eased his slippers on and stood up, supporting himself on the couch. Come on, he said, let's eat some. And hopped off to the kitchen. The boy followed.

They sat down to a breakfast of eggs and grits, biscuits and pork tenderloin and huge cups of coffee. The coffee was black and bitter and there was no milk or sugar on the table. The boy sipped it slowly, watched the man. The woman didn't eat with them. She hovered about the edge of the table resupplying eggs and biscuits to their plates, filling their cups. The man didn't say anything until he had finished except that from time to time he would nudge a plate toward the boy and frown and grunt, urging him to eat. He finished off with biscuits and dark honey and got up from the table. In a few minutes he was back with coats and boots and handed a set to the boy. Come on, he said, I got somethin to show you you might like. The boy pulled on the coat and stepped into the cavernous brogans and they went out the kitchen door into the new morning, the air clear and cold as springwater, shreds of mist lifting off the mountain above them and light pouring through the gap like a millrace. The man hobbled ahead of him to a smokehouse where he pulled a bent nail from the wood and swung out the door, hinge, hasp, lock, and all, and went in. Come on, he said. The boy followed him into the musty gloom. Hello, gal, the man said. The air was rife and fetid with dog smells. Sounds of snuffling. Thin mewlings from somewhere in the corner. A small hound poked her face around the man's knee and looked up at him. This here's Lady, the man said. Lady sniffed at his billowing trousers.

He could see now: a broken lantern swung from a beam, a clutter of tools, a grindstone, an anvil fashioned from a section of rail . . . The man was squatting in the corner, the hound skitting nervously behind his back, poking her nose under his arm. She got around him and settled in a pile of crokersacks and he could see the puppies then too over the man's shoulder. They crawled over each other and fell to nursing. Lady blinked her mild hound eyes and gazed at the roof.

The man picked out one and handed it to him. He took it, the fat slick little belly filling his palm, legs dangling, took it and looked at the quiet and already sad eyes, the pushed-in puppy face with the foolish ears.

Four weeks old, the man was saying. That's the best'n, but you can pick whichever one you want.

Do what?

His daddy's a blooded bluetick—half bluetick half walker, the pups. Makes as good a treedog as they is goin. You like that'n?

Yessir, he said.

Well, he's yourn then. You can take him home with ye in about another month, say.

Jefferson Gifford thumbed his galluses onto his shoulders, took a last swallow of coffee from the still full earthenware cup and crossed with heavy boot-tread the curling linoleum of the kitchen floor to the rear entranceway where he took down his hat and jacket from a peg.

A Plymouth? he repeated.

Legwater was buttoning his coat. That's what he said. I ain't been down there. All I know is he said it was a Plymouth. He come straight to my place on account of it was on his milk route and he ast for me to call you. So I jest come on over. He said it was a Plymouth.

Gifford adjusted his hat and opened the door. Well, come on, he said. I sure never heard of nobody hauling whiskey in a Plymouth.

Ain't you goin to call the Sheriff?

Reckon I'll see what all it is I'm callin him about first, Gifford said.

They parked the car just beyond the creek and climbed through the wire fence and walked along slow, studying the swath the car had cut through the brush and small trees. It had cleared the fence completely, peeling a limb from a cottonwood that grew by the bridge, and come to earth some thirty feet from the road. It was upside down in the creek against the far bank and facing back the way it came. Gifford couldn't see anything yet but the undercarriage, but he knew it wasn't a Ford this time by the two semi-elliptic springs at the rear axle. They had to go back to the road and cross the bridge to get to the car. It was smashed up against some roots on the bank and they could see the glass leaking from the trunk lid.

Later when they got a truck down and winched the wreck out the lid fell off and glass poured into the creek —someone said later for thirty minutes—for a long time anyway. There were even two or three jars unbroken, which pleased Gifford—evidence, he said . . .

It was a Plymouth, a 33 coupe; there was a hole in

the right front tire you could put three fingers in. Other than that there was nothing remarkable about it except that it was wrecked in Red Branch with the remains of a load of whiskey in the back end.

Gifford examined the ground carefully, walking back and forth along the bank as if he had lost something there. He had written the license number down on a slip of paper but on looking closer saw that they were last year's plates repainted and threw the paper away in disgust.

Looks to me like he'd of been hurt, Legwater was saying.

They.

They what?

Them, Gifford said. They's two of em.

You mean tracks? Them's most likely Oliver's; he come down to see was they anybody hurt . . .

Cept he never clumb down into the creek to . . . See? Here . . . Gifford paused, staring at the ground. After a long minute he looked up at Legwater. Earl, he said, I reckon you're right.

Figured I was . . .

Yep. The othern wadn't in the car. He jest come along and got whoever was in out.

It wadn't Oliver, Legwater persisted. He never even seen nobody around when he come by. He . . .

Ain't talkin about him, the constable said. Come on, if you're ready.

It had begun to rain a little by then.

Believe it may warm up for a spell, Gifford said. If it don't turn snow.

In the store the old men gathered, occupying for endless hours the creaking milkcases, speaking slowly and with conviction upon matters of profound inconsequence, eying the dull red bulb of the stove with their watery vision. Shrouded in their dark coats they had a vulturous look about them, their faces wasted and thin, their skin dry and papery as a lizard's. John Shell, looking like nothing so much as an ill-assembled manikin of bones on which clothes were hung in sagging dusty folds, his wrists protruding like weathered sticks from his flapping prelate sleeves, John Shell unhinged his toothless jaw with effort, a slight audible creaking sound, to speak his one pronouncement: It ain't so much that as it is one thing'n another.

An assemblage of nods to this. In the glass cases roaches scuttled, a dry rattling sound as they traversed the candy in broken ranks, scaled the glass with licoriced feet, their segmented bellies yellow and flat. Summer and winter they patrolled the candy case, inspected hand-kerchiefs, socks, cigars. Occasionally too they invaded the meat case, a medicinal white affair rusted from sweat where the lower edge of the glass was mortised, so that brown stains like tobacco spit or worse seeped down the enamel, but they soon perished here from the cold. Their corpses lay in attitudes of repose all along the little scupper to the front of the case.

Leaning against the case John Wesley could see the car pull in alongside the rusty orange gas pump and the two men get out. When they came through the door the nasal clacking voices paused, the chorus of elders looking up, down, back to the stove. Some fumbled knives from their overalls and fell to whittling idly on their milkcases. John Shell struggled to his feet, opened the stove door with kerchiefed hand, dropped in a small chunk of coal from the hod. A draft of sparks scurried upwards. He spat assertively at them and clanked the loose iron door closed.

The two men crossed to the dope box in close order,

on the raw subflooring their steps heavy and martial. They selected their drinks and the taller man came over to the counter and spun down a dime. The other one closed the lid and hiked himself up on the box where he sat taking little sips of his drink and smirking strangely at the old men.

John Shell turned to the man at the counter and said, Howdy, Gif.

Howdy, said Gifford, nodding in general to the group. He took a drink of his dope.

Mr Eller came from his chair by the meat block and rang up the dime. Gifford said Howdy to him too and he grunted and went back to his chair taking with him a newspaper from the counter.

Warmin up, Gifford said. Outside the rain had stopped and a cold wind feathered the red water puddles in front of the store. He tilted his head and drank again. A fly rattled electrically against the front window. The fire cricked and moaned in the stove.

Gifford hoisted his dope to eye-level, examined it, his mouth pursed about the unswallowed liquid, swirling the bottle slowly, studying viscosity and bead, suspicious of foreign matter. In the folds of flesh beneath his chin his Adam's apple rose and fell.

See where somebody lost a old Plymouth down in the creek, he said.

A few looked up. That a fact, someone said.

Yessir, said Gifford. Seems a shame.

Legwater, the county humane officer, finished now with his drink, sat leaning forward, hands palm-down-ward, sitting on his fingers—an attitude toadlike but for his thinness and the spindle legs dangling over the side of the box. He was swinging them out, banging his heels against the drink case. A longlegged and emaciated toad, then. He kept leering and smirking but no one paid

him any attention. Most of the old men had been there
the day he shot two dogs behind the store with a .22
rifle, one of them seven times, it screaming and dragging
itself along the fence in the field below the forks while
a cluster of children stood watching until they too began
screaming.

He said, Sure does . . . brightly, enjoying himself.

Gifford passed him a sharp glance sideways and he
hushed and fell to watching his heels bounce.

I don't reckon anybody knows whose car that is, do
they, Gifford went on.

A few of the elders seemed to be dozing. The fly
buzzed at the glass.

I got a towtruck comin to take it on in to town. Sure
would like to get that car to the rightful owner.

What kind of car did you say it was? It was the boy
leaning against the meat case who spoke.

Gif drained the last of his dope with studied indifference, set the bottle carefully on the counter. He looked
at the boy, then he looked at the boy's feet.

You always wear them slippers, son?

The boy didn't look down. He started to answer, but
he could feel the cords in his throat sticking. He coughed
and cleared his throat noisily. His feet felt huge.

Them ain't enough shoes for wet weather, Gifford
said. Then he was moving across the floor. Legwater
eased himself down from the drink box and fell in behind him. At the door Gif stopped, the door half open,
studying something obliquely overhead. Yessir, he said,
looks like it's fixin to clear off. Legwater hovered behind
him like some dark and ominous bird.

Well, we'll see ye, Gifford said.

By the meat block Mr Eller dozed with his paper. He
had not looked up nor did he now. Come back, he said.

And they were gone. The fly rattled again at the

window. The congress of ancients about the stove stirred one by one. The boy stood uneasily by the meat case. Some of the old men were rolling smokes with their brown papery hands. It was very quiet. He went to the door and stood there for a while. Then he left.

Her first high yelp was thin and clear as the air itself, its tenuous and diminishing echoes sounding out the coves and hollows, trebling to a high ring like the last fading note of a chime glass. He could hear the boy breathing in the darkness at his elbow, trying to breathe quietly, listening too hard. She sounded again and he stood and touched the boy's shoulder lightly. Let's go, he said.

The strung-out ringing yelps came like riflefire. The boy was on his feet. Has she treed yet? he asked.

No. She's jest hit it now. Then he added: She's close though, hot. He started down the steep hummock on which they had been resting, through a maze of small pines whose polished needles thick on the ground made the descent a series of precarious slides from trunk to trunk until they got to the gully at the bottom, a black slash in the earth beyond which he could see nothing although he knew there was a field there, pitched sharply down to the creek some hundred yards further on. He dropped into the gully, heard the beaded rush of sliding dirt as the boy followed, came up the other side and started out through the field at a jog-trot, the heavy weeds popping and his corduroys setting up a rhythmic zip-zip as he ran.

The cottonwoods at the creek loomed up stark and pale out of the darkness; he crossed a low wreck of barbed wire, heard again the resonant creak of the rusty staples in the checked and split cedar post as the boy crossed behind him. They were in the woods above the creek then, rattling through the stiff frosted leaves.

Lady's sharp trail-call still broke excitedly off to their right. They moved out under the dark trees, through a stand of young cedars gathered in a clearing, vespertine figures, rotund and druidical in their black solemnity. When the man reached the far side, the woods again, he stopped and the boy caught up with him.

Which way is she going? He was trying not to sound winded.

The man paused for just a moment more. Then he said, Same way he is—motioning loosely with his hand. His back melted into the darkness again. The boy moved after him, keeping his feet high, following the sound of the brittle leaves. Their path angled down toward the creek and he could hear at intervals the rush of water, high now after the rain, like the rumble of a distant freight passing.

Watch a log, the man called back to him. He jumped just in time, half stumbled over the windfall trunk, lost his balance, ricocheted off a sapling, went on, holding his head low, straining to see. Trees appeared, slid past with slow gravity before folding again into the murk beyond. They were climbing now, a long rise, and when he came over the crest he caught a glimpse of the figure ahead of him, framed darkly for an instant against the glaucous drop of sky. Below him he could make out the course of the creek. They dipped into a low saddle in the ridge, rose again, and the man was no longer there. He stopped and listened. Lady's clear voice was joined by another, lower and less insistent. She was much closer now, quartering down, coming closer. He could follow her progress, listening between the explosions of his breath. Then she stopped.

There was a moment of silence, then the other dog yapped once. Sounds of brush crashing. Two wild yelps just off to his right and then a concussion of water. A low voice at his side said: He's got her in the creek, come on. The man started down the side of the hill, the boy behind him, and out onto a small flat set in the final slope to the creek and dominated by a thick beech tree. Something was coming down from the ridge above them and they halted. A long shadow swept past in a skitter of leaves and on toward the creek bank. There was one short chopped bark and then a splash. They followed, sidling down the slope and out along the bank where the water gathered a thin membranous light by which they could see, directed by frantic surging sounds and low intermittent growls, some suggestion of figures struggling there, and the new dog striking out in the water now to join them. The fight moved down, out in deep water and under the shadow of the far bank. The snarls stopped and there was only the desperate rending of water.

A light blinked through the trees to their right, went out, appeared again, bobbing, unattached and eerie in the blackness. They could hear the dry frosted crack of sticks and brush, muted voices. The light darted out, peered again suddenly down upon them, sweeping an arc along the edge of the creek.

Howdy, a voice said.

Cas?

Yeah . . . that you, Marion?

Bring that light; they're in the creek.

They came down the slope, four dismembered legs hobbling in the swatch of light as they descended.

Thow your light, Sylder said.

They came alongside, dispensing an aura of pipesmoke and doghair. The shorter one was working the beam slowly over the creek. Whereabouts? he said.

Down some. Howdy, Bill.

Howdy, the other said. In the glare emanating from the flashlight their breath was smoke-white, curling, clinging about their heads in a vaporous canopy. The oval of the flashbeam scudded down the glides against the far bank, passed, backed, came to rest on the combatants clinching in the icy water, the coon's eyes glowing red, pin points, his fur wetly bedraggled and his tail swaying in crestfallen buoyancy on the current. The big dog was circling him warily, trudging the water with wearying paws and failing enthusiasm. They could see Lady's ear sticking out from under the coon's front leg, and then her hindquarters bobbed up, surging through the face of the creek with a wild flash of tail and sinking back in a soundless swirl.

Cas swung the beam to shore, scrabbled up a handful of rock and handed the light to the other man. Hold it on him, he said. He scaled a rock at the coon. It cut a slow arc in the beam and pitched from sight with a muffled slurp. The big hound started for shore and Lady's tail had made another desperate appearance when the second rock, a flitting shadow, curving, flashed water under the coon's face.

He turned loose and struck out downstream, stroking with the current. The big dog, on the other bank now, had set up a pitiful moaning sound, pacing, the man with the light calling to him in a hoarse and urgent voice, Hunt im up, boy, hunt im up. He turned to the men. He's skeered of rocks, he explained.

Hush a minute, Sylder said, taking the light from him. She was already some thirty yards below them. When the light hit her she turned her head back and her eyes came pale orange, ears fanned out and floating, treading the water down before her with a tired and grim determination. She had her mouth turned up at the corners in a macabre and ludicrous grin as if to keep out the water.

Ho, gal, Sylder called. Ho, gal. They were moving down the creek too, raking through the brush. She's fixin to drownd herself, someone said.

Ho, gal, Ho . . .

He never even felt the water. He couldn't hear them any more, hadn't heard them call since he left them somewhere back up the creek when he hit the bullbriers full tilt, not feeling them either, aware only of them pulling at his coat and legs like small hands trying to hold him. Then he was over the bank, feet reaching for something and finally skewing on the slick mud, catapulting him in a stifflegged parabola down and out into the water, arms flailing, but not falling yet, not until he had already stopped, teetering thigh-deep, and took a first step out into the current where he collapsed forward like a shot heron.

But he didn't even feel it. When he came up again he

was in water past his waist, the soft creek floor squirming away beneath his feet as if he were walking the bodies of a colony of underwater creatures clustered there. He could see a little better now. There was no light on the bank and he thought: I come down too far. And no voices, only the sounds of the creek chattering and rocking past all around him. Then he went in again, over his head this time, and came up treading water and with something heavy pushing against his chest. He got his arms under it and lifted. Lady's head came up and her eyes rolled at him dumbly. He reached and got hold of her collar, the creek bottom coming up and sliding off under his feet, falling backwards now with the dog rolling over him and beginning to struggle, until his leg hit a rock and he reached for it and steadied himself and rose again and began to flounder shoreward with the dog in tow.

They came with the light and Sylder looked at him huddled in the willows, still holding the dog. He didn't say anything, just disappeared into the woods, returning in a few minutes with a pile of brush and dead limbs.

One of the men was kneeling with him and stroking the dog, examining her. She looks all right, he said, don't she, son?

He couldn't get his mouth open so he just nodded. He was beyond cold now, paralyzed.

The other man said: Son, you goin to take your death. We better get you home fore you freeze settin right there.

He nodded again. He wanted to get up but he couldn't bear the rub of his clothes where he moved.

Sylder had the fire going by then, a great crackling sound as the dry brush took, orange light leaping among the trees. He could see him in silhouette moving about, feeding the blaze. Then he came back. He gathered the quivering hound up in one arm and motioned for the boy to follow. You come over here, he said. And get them clothes off.

He got up then and labored stiffly after them.

Sylder put the hound by the fire and turned to the boy. Lemme have that coat, he said.

The boy peeled off the leaden mackinaw and handed it over to him. He passed it around the trunk of a sapling, gathered the ends up in his hands and twisted what looked to be a gallon of water out of the loose wool. Then he hung it over a bush. When he looked back the boy was still standing there.

Get em off, he said.

He started pulling his clothes off, the man taking from him in turn shirt and trousers, socks and drawers, wringing them out and hanging them over a pole propped on forks before the fire. When he was finished he stood naked, white as a slug in the cup of firelight. Sylder took off his coat and threw it to him.

Put it on, he said. And get your ass over here in front of the fire.

The two men were behind him in the woods; he could hear them crashing about, see the wink of their light. One of them came back toting a huge log and dropped it on the fire. A flurry of sparks ascended, flared, lost in the smoke pulling at the bare limbs overhead, returned tracing their slow fall redly through the dark trees downwind.

He sat in a trampled matting of vines, the long coat just covering his buttocks. Sylder made a final adjustment to the pole and came over. He lit a cigarette and stood regarding him.

Kind of cool, ain't it? he said.

The boy looked up at him. Cool enough, he said.

The clothes had begun to steam, looking like some esoteric game quartered and smoking on the spit.

Then he said, What'd you do with the coon?

Coon?

Yeah. The coon.

Goddamn, the boy said, I never saw the coon.

Oh, Sylder said. But his voice was giving him away. Hell, I figured you'd of got the coon too.

Shoo, the boy said. Over his teeth the firelight rippled and danced.

The two men were warming their hands at the fire, the shorter one grinning goodnaturedly at the boy. The other hound had appeared, hovering suddenly at the rim of light and snuffling at the steaming wool and then slouching past them with nervous indifference, the slack hound grace, to where Lady lay quietly peering across her paws into the fire. He nosed at her and she raised her head to look at him with her sad red eyes. He stood so for a minute, looking past her, then stepped neatly over her and melted silently into the black wickerwork of the brush. The other man moved over to her and reached down to pat her head. One ear was mangled and crusting with blood.

Coon's hard on a walker, he said. Walker's got too much heart. Old redbone like that—he motioned toward the blackness that encircled them—he'll quit if it gets too rough. Little old walker though—he addressed the dog now—she jest got too much heart, ain't she?

When Sylder let him out of the car his clothes were still wet. You better scoot in there fast, he told him. Your maw raise hell with you?

Naw, he said, she'll be asleep.

Well, Sylder said. We'll go again. You got to stay out of the creek though. Here, I got to get on. My old lady'll be standin straight up.

All right, we'll see ye. He let the door fall.

Night, Sylder said. The car pulled away trailing ropy plumes of smoke, the one red taillight bobbing. He turned toward the house, lightless and archaic among the crumbling oaks, crossed the frosted yard. His shadow swept upward to the lean-to roof, dangled from a limb, upward again, laced with branches, stood suddenly upon the roof. He slid downward over the eaves and disappeared in the black square of the gable window.

III

Some time after midnight on the twenty-first of December it began to snow. By morning in the gray spectral light of a brief and obscure winter sun the fields lay dead-white and touched with a phosphorous glow as if producing illumination of themselves, and the snow was still wisping down thickly, veiling the trees beyond the creek and the mountain itself, falling softly, and softly, faintly sounding in the immense white silence.

On that morning the old man rose early and stared long out at the little valley. Nothing moved. The snow fell ceaselessly. When he pushed the screendoor it dragged heavily in the drifts packed on the porch and against the house. He stood there in his shirtsleeves watching the great wafers of snow list and slide, dodging the posts at the corner of the house. It was very cold.

The hiss of the coffeepot boiling over on the stove brought him in again.

All day it darkened so that when night came no one could tell just when it had come about. Yet the snow fell, undiminished. Windless, pillowed in silence, down-sifting . . . No one was about. All the dogs were quiet. In his house the old man lit a lamp and settled back in a stout rocker near the stove. He selected a magazine from a rack alongside, an ancient issue of *Field and Stream*, limp and worn, the pages soft as chamois, spread it on his lap and began to leaf through it who knew it now almost by heart—stories, pictures, advertisements. From time to time he could hear scuffling sounds beneath him, scratchings in the darkness under the floor where Scout turned uneasily in his nest of rotting sacks.

He turned the pages for a while and then got up and went to the kitchen where from a high cupboard above the tapless sink he fetched down a molasses jar near filled with a viscous brickcolored liquid opaque as clay. He screwed off the cap, took a clean jelly jar from the sideboard and poured it full. Then he went back to his chair, settled the drink on its broad arm, adjusted the magazine in his lap and began to rock gently back and forth, the liquid in the glass lapping sluggishly with the motion. Now and again he took a sip, staining the white stubble beneath his lip a deep maroon. The oil-lamp glowed serenely at its image, a soft corolla, inflaming the black window-glass where a curled and withered spider dangled from a dusty thread.

The old man rocked, dwarflike in his ponderous chair. He seemed to be weighing some dark problem posed in the yellowed pages before him.

Toward late morning a rooster called and the old man's window blushed in a soft wash of rose. He slept and color drained from the glass and the east paled ash-gray. The rooster called once again, questioningly, and shortly the old man jerked awake in his chair, knocking the jelly glass to the floor where it rolled about woodenly.

He peered through the hazy light of the room. It was morning, the lamp out and the stove too, and he found himself stiff and shivering with the cold, rubbing his eyes now, then his back. He rose gingerly and opened the door of the stove, poked among the feathery ashes. He went to the window and looked out. The snow had stopped. Scout was standing in snow to his belly, gazing out at the fantastic landscape with his bleary eyes. Across the yard, brilliant against the façade of pines beyond, a cardinal shot like a drop of blood.

There were three of them coming up the trackless road past the house, and two dogs. One of them carried a rabbit, holding it loosely by the hind legs, its head jerking limply as they went. The other two carried guns and the boy knew one of them. He hadn't seen him since school started in September.

They were talking and gesturing and they didn't notice him standing there in the yard so he moved out toward the road, making for the mailbox, plopping his feet into the dazzling and unbroken drifts. The one carrying the rabbit had his feet wrapped—wound and encased in burlap sacks to the knee and held with twine. He saw him coming and then Warn turned and saw him too and waved.

Heyo, John Wesley.

Howdy, he said, sliding down the bank.

He met Warn Pulliam in the summer, headed toward the pond one afternoon when he saw the buzzard circling low over Tipton's field and noticed that there was a string looping down from its leg. He came up through the field to the crest of the hill and there was Warn holding the other end of the string while the buzzard soared with lazy unconcern above his head.

Howdy, Warn said.

Howdy. He was looking up at the buzzard. What you doin?

Ah, jest flyin the buzzard some. He cain't get up lessen they's some wind. So when we get a little wind I gen'ly fly him some.

Where'd you get him, he asked. The back of his neck was already beginning to ache from staring up at the wheeling bird.

Caught him in a steel trap. You want to see him?

Sure.

He pulled the bird out of the sky by main force, heaving on the cord against the huge and ungiving expanse of wing, lowering him circle by circle until he brought him to earth. There the buzzard flopped about on its one good leg and came to rest eying them truculently, beady eyes unblinking in the naked and obscene-looking skull.

Turkey buzzard, Warn explained. They's the ones got red heads.

Where do you keep him?

Been keepin him in the smokehouse, he said.

Don't nobody care for you to keep him?

Naw. The old lady set up a fuss but I told her I was goin to bring him in the house and learn him to set at table and that calmed her down some. Here, don't get too close or he'll puke on ye. He puked on Rock and Rock like to never got over it—stit won't have nothin to do with him. Don't nobody think much of him I reckon but me. I like him cause he's about a mean son of a bitch and twice as ugly. What's your name?

The two dogs were beagles, shortlegged and frantic, leaping in and out of the chest-high fall of snow, or plowing their noses through it and furrowing snow up and past their ears, their tails spinning, then looking up with white brows and whiskers, gnomic and hoary-faced as little old men.

Where you-all goin? he asked them.

T'wards the quarry, Warn said. Come on go with us—I got me a skunk in a hole I got to get out. This here's Johnny Romines—motioning at the tall boy with the shotgun—and that there's Boog.

Howdy, he said. They nodded.

We done got us a rabbit, Boog said, holding up the snow-dusted and stiffening quarry. Johnny shot him in the field yonder.

The dogs circled him, sniffing his cuff. Them's Johnny's dogs, Boog added. Rabbit dogs. Bugles.

Beagles, idjit, Warn said.

Yeah, Boog said. Them's what they are.

Where's Rock? the boy asked.

He's layin up under the house still lickin his foot where he accidental stepped in the snow this mornin. Cain't get him to stir a stump. Sides he won't run rabbits noway. He's a bear dog.

I got me a dog now, he told them. Half bluetick and half walker. Makes as good a tree dog as they is goin. They were moving up the road, the beagles for outriders prancing and frisking.

You run him? Boog asked.

Naw. He's jest a pup. I been keepin him with a feller over on Henderson Valley Road raises dogs. He's the one give him to me.

You don't need no more excuse to run wild at night. That was what she said to him standing there in the kitchen with the pup under his arm. She must be a pis-

*tol, Sylder said when he returned with it, embarrassed,
explaining why he couldn't keep it. Don't make no dif-
ference though. He's stit yourn; you jest keep him here
is all and come get him any time you've a mind to.*

I got me a old musket at home belonged to my great-
grandaddy, Boog said. It's nigh on long as me my own
sef.

They left the road and crossed a field dotted with
scrub cedars, the beagles coursing now and Johnny
Romines calling to them to hunt. He and Warn trampled
the brush piled all down a rock draw and scouted the
frozen drainage ditches but no rabbits appeared. They
crossed a fence and came out onto the railroad, following it south across the white quilted fields, the sun on
them now glinting and the last traces of icefog dis-
persing in myriad blue crystals on the shining air.

At the sinkhole they stopped and skittered down the
bank to test the ice; it was black and evil-looking and
woven with sticks and weeds. The beagles came to the
edge and whined, pawing tentatively. After a while they
came out too and rushed wheeling and sliding in a game
of tag, their hindquarters spinning from under them as
they turned. Boog couldn't skate because of his feet
being wrapped so he sat on the bank holding the rabbit
and watching them. Later he built a fire, making a plat-
form of hickory bark and piling dead cedar branches on
top and they came and sat around it.

This here's where Johnny caught the bullfrog, Warn
said. Right over yander off the end of that log. By the
ass in a mousetrap.

How'd he do that? John Wesley asked.

He bet me a dope on it. I seen him come by the house
with this mousetrap on a piece of bailin wire. Said he
was fixin to catch him a bullfrog. We come on over and
he set it on the end of that log there and then we went

on to the store. I thought the poor bastard had done lost
his rabbit-assed mind . . .

Johnny Romines grinned. He told everybody in the
store, he said.

Yeah, we all like to of fell out laughin. So the son of
a bitch bets me a dope he's caught one by the time we
come back and sure as hell there he is. Pinched right by
the ass. I like to never got over it. And wouldn't nothin
do but we come straight back to the store frog trap and
all and me buy him the dope right there.

It's a old Indian trick, said Boog.

What's that?

Puttin bark down like that. To lay your fire on.

When he reached the fence he rested again, removed
his gloves and blew into his cupped hands. Along the
face of the mountain and down the valley floor guns
were sounding, echoing in diminishing reiteration. The
trees were all encased in ice, limbless-looking where their
black trunks rose in aureoles of lace, bright seafans shimmering in the wind and tinkling with an endless bell-like
sound, a carillon in miniature, and glittering shards of
ice falling in sporadic hail everywhere through the woods
and marking the snow with incomprehensible runes.
Something flicked rapid and invisibly past and struck
with a soft pock into the bark of a poplar above him.
The thin spat and whine of a rifle followed.

The old man paid no attention. He pulled his gloves
on, gathered the wire in one hand and stepped through,
the posts on the downhill side jiggling where they dangled in their wires like sticks in a spiderweb, the earth
having long been washed from about their moorings.
Some dogs were trailing and after a while he could see
them below him where the last finger of bleak trees

reached into a cut and met the barren fields, the dogs coming out from behind the timber, moving slow and diminutive, their voices small as a child's horn, two of them. They dipped into the cut and swarmed up the other side and out, across the fields, their brown and white shapes losing definition in the confectionary landscape of mudclods and snow until only their motion was discernible, like part of the ground itself rumoring upheaval.

He went slowly, the snow heavier now, drifted and billowing in the honeysuckle and breaking it down into the path so that he had to skirt below it in places, teetering with edged steps along the incline, uncovering in his footsteps wet patches of leaf black as swampwater, not even frozen. When he reached the top of the mountain, the road curving away in a white swath through the trees, he paused to brush the snow from his shoulders and turn out the lumps of ice gathered in his cuffs. He plowed his way down the drifts some hundred yards and re-entered the woods to the other side, carrying in his hand now the huge handleless knife forged from an old millfile, receding among the small trees in his stooped and shambling gait, apparitional, a strange yuletide assassin.

A quarter hour later he emerged back into the road again still carrying the knife and dragging behind him a small cedar tree. At the curve below the orchard he stopped and looked back, then relegated the knife to some place in the folds of his coat and shouldered the tree. A little further on he entered the woods again, trace of a path or road leading off to the right. This time he was gone for only a few minutes. When he came back, unburdened of the tree now, he followed his tracks to where he had first come onto the road and so disappeared once more into the woods, down the slope of the mountain the way by which he came.

They threaded their way over the jumbled limestone of the quarry, Warn in the lead, until they came to the cave.

It don't look like much, Johnny Romines said.

It opens up inside, Warn said. Here, let me hang him up here and I'll show ye. He wedged the skunk in the fork of a sapling and then disappeared down into the earth, crawling on hands and knees through a small hole beneath the rocks. They followed one by one, the stiff winter nettles at the cave door rattling viperously against the legs of their jeans. Inside they struck matches and Warn took a candlestub from a crevice and lit it, the calcined rock taking shape, tonsiled roof and flowing concavity, like something gone partly to liquid and frozen back again misshapen and awry, their shadows curling threatfully up the walls among the dried and mounded bat-droppings. They studied the inscriptions etched in the soft and curdcolored stone, hearts and names, archaic dates, crudely erotic hieroglyphs—the bulbed phallus and strange centipedal vulva of small boys' imaginations.

They followed the strip of red clay that traced the cave floor into another and larger room, hooted at their lapping echoes, their laughter rebounding in hollow and mocking derision. Water dripped ceaselessly, small ping and spatter on stone. The two dogs hung close to them, stepping nervously.

This'n here's the biggest room, Warn said. Then I got me a secret room on back with a rock in front of it so you cain't see it. Then they's a tunnel goes back, but

I ain't never been to the end of it. Ain't no tellin where-all it goes.

Boog came up dragging a load of dead limbs and presently they had a fire going in the center of the big room. This here is the way the cave-men used to do, Boog said.

They used to be cave-men hereabouts, said Warn. Pre-storic animals too. They's a tush over on the other side of the mountain stickin out of some rock what's long as your leg. Ain't no way to get to it lessen you had ropes or somethin.

Johnny Romines took out a packet of tobacco and rolled a cigarette. Boog borrowed it and rolled one too and they sat smoking in long steady pulls. Which'd you rather be, Boog asked John Wesley, white or Indian?

I don't know, the boy said. White I reckon. They always whipped the Indians.

Boog tipped the ash from his cigarette with his little finger. That's so, he said. That's a point I hadn't studied.

I got Indian in me, Johnny Romines said.

Boog's half nigger, said Warn.

I ain't done it, Boog said.

You said niggers was good as whites.

I never. What I said was *some* niggers is good as *some* whites is what I said.

That what you said?

Yeah.

I had a uncle was a White-Cap, Johnny Romines said. You ought to hear him on niggers. He claims they're kin to monkeys.

John Wesley didn't say anything. He'd never met any niggers.

Tell John Wesley here about the time we dynamited the birds, Warn said. This is last Christmas, he explained.

His daddy give him a electric train one time and they got it out for his little brother.

Johnny Romines told it, slowly, smiling from time to time. They had wired the transformer of the train to a dynamite cap stolen from the quarry shack and buried the cap in the snow.

We had us a long piece of lightwire, he said, and we set in the garage with the transformer all hooked up. Warn here claimed it wouldn't work. Well, we'd sprinkled breadcrumbs all round over where the cap was buried out in the yard and directly you couldn't see for the birds. I told Warn to thow the switch.

Goddamn but it come a awful blast, said Warn. I eased the switch on over and then BALOOM! They's a big hoop of snow jumped up in the yard like when you thow a flat rock in the pond and birds goin ever which way mostly straight up. I remember we run out and you could see pieces of em strung all out in the yard and hangin off the trees. And feathers. God, I never seen the like of feathers. They was stit fallin next mornin.

Lord, whispered Boog, I'd of liked to of seen that.

John Wesley had begun to cough. Ain't it gettin kindly smoky in here to you? he asked. Above their heads smoke roiled and lowered and they noticed they could no longer see the walls of the cave.

Believe it is some, Warn said. He stood up and was closed from sight by the smoke. Hell's bells, he said, let's get out of here.

This is the way the cave-men done it, Boog said.

Cave-men be damned, we're fixin to get barbycued.

They crawled and stumbled to the mouth of the cave—a shifting patch of murky light weaving beyond the smoke combers, came red-eyed and weeping from their crypt, their jacket fronts encrusted with slick red mud. When they had dried their eyes and could see again they were in some volcanic and infernal under-region, the whole of the quarry woods wrapped in haze and smoke boiling up out of the rocky ground from every cleft and fissure.

Mr Eller stood at the counter and watched them come in, the clothes steaming on the backs of the men as they stomped off the slush from their shoes and stood about the stove making cigarettes with chilled fingers, the stove popping and whistling with the snow-wetted coal, the women excited with the cold, making their pur-chases with deliberation, some towing small children about in the folds of their skirts, leaving again, young boys with shotguns and rifles buying shells not by the box but by fours and sixes and lending to the bustle a purposeful and even militant air. He rang the money up in the cash register or marked it in his credit books.

Odor of smoke and cold, wet clothing and meat cooking. The snow was falling again and they watched it. Lord, Mr Eller said, reckon it's ever goin to quit.

Boog and Johnny Romines came in with a rabbit and they each got a dope.

Whereabouts you get him, Johnny? Mr Eller asked.

Over on the creek.

Warn Pulliam caught a skunk in a hole, Boog said.

That right? How's he smell?

He don't smell too purty.

The men laughed. He's a fat'n, one said, nodding toward the rabbit. How's them pups run? Purty good?

Purty good little old rabbit dogs, Johnny said. They jumped two more but I never got a clear shot.

Them's beagles, said Boog.

. . .

The old man came out on the pike road at the gap where the Green Fly Inn had stood. There was no trace of the inn now but the black and limbless pine trunk that stood in the hollow. Snow had started again, dropping like a veil over the valley or riding the wind through the gap, stinging his face a little. He walked down until he came to the Twin Fork road and took it into the Hopper and homeward. From a lightwire overhead, dangling head downward and hollowed to the weight of ashened feathers and fluted bones, a small owl hung in an attitude of forlorn exhortation, its wizened talons locked about the single strand of wire. It stared down from dark and empty sockets, penduluming softly in the bitter wind.

At the head of the hollow there was a springhouse and they stopped to drink, the water green and pulsing up from the rocks where a scalloped fringe of ice jutted just above the waterline.

I figured to set here, Warn said, but they's too many people come by and you'd get your traps stole. Come on I'll show you where I got my culvert-set. He dipped up another mouthful of the numbing water, took the rifle and trap and handed the skunk to the younger boy. He don't smell so bad out in the air, he said. The old lady'll pitch a hissy when she gets a whiff of me though.

They came out on the road and crossed to the other side where the creek ran. Warn got down on one knee and peered back through the culvert under the road where the spring run trickled through.

It don't never freeze in here, he said. I done caught me one muskrat here but what I'm lookin for is a mink. See? I got the trap jest back inside where nobody won't notice it.

The boy peered into the dark tunnel, the water loping

slowly down the corrugated metal and flaring where it passed over the trap.

I seen mink sign here back in the fall and some lately, Warn said. They's mink on Stock Creek too. Used to be some on Red Branch but they ain't any more is how come I don't trap it no more. You ready to go?

See, they ain't been no cars in here yet, Warn said. Ain't but jest a few people live over here in the holler and mostly they ain't got cars. You see that house up yander?

He looked where Warn pointed. Set back off the road was a squat saddle-roofed structure with a thin wisp of smoke swirling and circling about the top of the chimney.

That's where Garland Hobie lives, he told him. You mess around there you get your ass shot off.

How come?

On account of he makes whiskey, Warn said. Him and his old lady. Here. I'll show you somethin directly.

Beyond the curve of the road there was an old frame church and Warn pointed it out. See that church? Well, that was a nigger church. They used to be a bunch of niggers lived in the holler and they built this here church and commenced singin and hollerin of a night till old man Hobie, he's dead now, he run em ever one off. He's been dead since afore you and me was born and they ain't none of em come back yet. That's how strong he was on niggers. They say Ef was even meaner'n the old man. He died right at the store back a few year ago. Jest got out of Brushy Mountain. Garland, he's meaner'n hell too. They raided em one time here back and he give em the old lady to take off to jail. His own mama. That's how bad he is. Then they's Uncle Ather lives up here—nodding ahead of them—he's a purty good old feller.

Is he your uncle?

Naw. Him and Grandaddy Pulliam worked together cuttin sleepers for the K S & E. So the old man always called him Uncle. He's purty old. Got a dog pret-near old as you and me both.

That's purty old, the boy said. How old is he, Uncle . . .

Uncle Ather? He must be ninety or better. He's older'n Grandaddy Pulliam and Grandaddy Pulliam's daddy fought in the Civil War. He owned a lot of land in Knox County and when the war was over they took it away from him on account of him bein a Confederate. Grandaddy Pulliam says they wouldn't even let nobody vote ceptin niggers and yankees.

Why was that?

On account of back then this was the North I reckon.

Late in the afternoon the old man was sweeping the snow from his front porch when he saw them coming up the road, two small figures dark against the unbroken fall of snow, laboring through the drifts. One of them was carrying a dead skunk. They came abreast of his mailbox and the taller one raised his hand. Heyo, Uncle Ather, he called.

The old man squinted his milkblue eyes against the glare. Hiram Pulliam's grandson. He grinned and waved them up and they came, toiling on the slope, bowlegged for a better grip in the snow, the Pulliam boy leaning on his rifle and the other one sliding and waving the skunk about in the air.

They sat around the stove with their shoes off, their socks steaming. The old man wrinkled his nose and laughed.

I believe you must of fit that there polecat hand to hand, he said.

Can you smell it? Warn said. I cain't smell it myself.

He had to crawl back in a hole to get him out, John Wesley said.

I crawled past where he was at, Warn said. I thought he was way on back and then I come to see the wire and it went off into a little side-hole, but I was already past it then. I was all hunkered up down in there and couldn't hardly turn around, but directly I got to where I could poke my pine knot in the side-hole there and I seen his eyes. I got my rifle turned around and aimed the best way I could and when I shot, it like to busted out my eardrums.

We could hear him shoot, John Wesley said. It sounded like a little old popgun or somethin from on the outside.

Well, when I shot he cut loose too. I mean it really steamed things up in there. I come scootin out hind-end first and we waited a while and then directly I went back and got holt of the wire and come draggin him out and he's shot between the eyes.

The old man laughed. That puts me in mind of a coon hunt I was on one time, he said. Feller with us shot a coon in a tree and it hung in a limb. So I helt the light and he went up after him. Time he got to the limb where the coon was at it come to life and made at him. He figured purty quick he didn't want no part of it, but stead of comin down he scooted up another limb and there he set. Ever time he made like he was comin down the coon'd go at him, growlin like a bear. Well, directly he got mad and he decided he'd come on down anyway. So here he come. He was goin to kick the coon off of the limb is what he hollered down to us. We had the lannern on him and could see purty good. He made two or three swipes at the coon and about that time the old coon latched on to his foot. I never heard the like of hollerin. He commenced swingin that coon around on the end of his toe and he got so took up with it he kindly eased up his holt on the tree. Well, wadn't but a few minutes one of us hollered to Look out! and here they come pilin down out of the tree. He hit the ground like a sack of feed and jest laid there and the dogs piled on to the coon and they commenced walkin all in his face and fightin till we got em kicked off. We thought he's dead, but directly he begun to breathe a little and his eyes to flitter some and we seen he wadn't hurt, jest the wind pooched out of him and scared purty bad. We all laughed considerable and he set there and cussed us, but he was a purty good old boy and I reckon he never helt it against us. I remember he used to tell it on his own sef for years and years and laugh jest like anybody.

The old man sighed. Used to be good coon huntin hereabouts, he said.

What about painters? Warn asked. Was that a painter was hollerin around here one time?

The old man leaned back in his rocker, a wise grin settling among his sagging skinfolds. Well now, he said. Shore, I remember that right well. Been about ten year ago I'd say. There followed a moment of silence in which he seemed to be contemplating with satyric pleasure some old deed. Then he crossed one knee over the other and leaned forward. Shore, he repeated, I heard it. Many's the time. Had folks stirred up and scared all of one summer. Yessir, stirred up a blue fog of speculatin.

What'd it sound like? the boy asked.

Oh, purty fierce . . .

Well, you reckon it was a painter?

Nope, the old man said.

After a minute Warn said, What was it?

The old man had begun to rock gently, a benign look upon his face, composed in wisdom, old hierophant savoring a favorite truth . . . He stopped and looked down at them. Well, I'll tell ye. It was a hoot-owl.

He studied their fallen faces, the hopeful incredulity. Yep, he said, a hoot-owl. One of them big'ns, screechin and a-hollerin on this mountain of summer evenins like any painter. They's folks said painter, folks said not. But I knowed what it was right along. So I let em do their speculatin and arguin . . . I recollect one evenin I was at the store gettin some things, late summer it was and nigh dark, bout eight o'clock I reckon, when it commenced hollerin. Well, I never said nothin. In a little bit it come again. Boys, I mean it got quiet in that store to where you could hear the ants in the candy jar. Stit I never let on nothin and after a while Bob Kirby—he's there—he hollered at me and he said, Hey! Uncle Ather. You fixin to walk crost that mountain tonight?

Well, I turned to him kind of surprised-like and I said, Why shore. A feller's got to get home sometime, and the best way he can. How come you to ast me that?

He jest looked at me for a minute, then he kind of grinned and he said, Cain't you hear that wampus cat?

Why, I said, shore I hear it. Anybody't wadn't deaf could hear that, I reckon.

Well, he kind of figured he had me then so he says, Ain't you skeered of painters, Uncle Ather?

Why shore, I says. Anybody ceptin a fool'd be skeered of one, a full-growed one leastways.

Then I never said nothin, jest went to the dope box and got me a dope and commenced drinkin it and lookin at my watch ever oncet in a while. I could see he was plenty puzzled and he tried to slip a grin to the rest of the fellers there once or twicet cept they wadn't grinnin and I reckon was more puzzleder'n he was. So he never said nothin neither, but after a while they's a young feller there, he piped up and ast me if that wadn't a full-growed one that was raisin all that hell out there. Well, about that time it come again, hollerin, and I looked at him and I said, They Lord God, son, I don't know what you'd do if a growed one was to squall. Why that ain't nothin there. But then course they ain't painters round like they used to be. Back fifty, sixty years ago they'd sing out back and forth crost these mountains all night of a summer till you got to where you couldn't sleep lessen you did hear em. But it takes a big old tom painter to set up a fuss. That there ain't nothin. I told him that and about that time shore enough that owl let out another screech couldn't of been a hundred yards off and I could see the hackles come up on his neck and on Bob Kirby's too.

I finished my dope and set it down and made like I was fixin to leave then and Kirby, he says, stit grinnin kind of, You mean, Uncle Ather, that you can tell one painter from anothern by its squall?

Well, I said, I don't reckon I can so good any more. He grinned right big at that.

But, I says, since I seen this'n t'other night I guess it jest don't worry me none.

Well, they all jumped up with somethin to ast then, how big it was and all. I was already half out the door, but I figured to give em somethin to think about while *they* walked home, so I turned to em and I says, Why it ain't more'n a kitten. It's right up here in the gap not even dusk-dark t'other night I seen it scoot crost the road. Old Scout was layin there on the concrete. Now he's fell off some of late but used to be he come a good bit higher'n my knee—to where you jest could straddle him, and weighed better'n a hunderd pound. So I looked around and I seen him there and I jest pointed to him and I said, Why he ain't a whole lot bigger'n Scout here, and said em a good night and went on.

Down the small panes of glass behind the old man's chair the sun lowered, casting his head in silhouette and illumining his white hair with a prophetic translucence. A little later he rose and went to the table and lit the lamp.

You boys care for some . . . here, jest a minute. He excused himself and went flapping off to the kitchen from where issued in a moment sounds of cupboards and glassware. When he came back he was carrying two glasses and a cup, a mason jar of some dark red liquid. Here, he said, handing them each a glass. He unscrewed the lid of the jar and poured their glasses. A heavy and evil-looking potion the color of iodine. Muskydine wine, he said. Bet you-all ain't never had none.

It beaded black and sinister in the soft lampglow. He settled himself in his rocker and filled his cup, watching them taste it.

Mighty fine, Warn said.

Yessir, said the boy.

They sipped their wine with the solemnity of communicants, troglodytes gathered in some firelit cave. The lamp guttered in a draft of wind and their shadows, ponderous and bearlike upon the wall, weaved in unison.

Uncle Ather, said the boy, was they really painters back then?

Warn's face, a harlequin mask etched in black and orange by the lamplight, turned to the old man. Tell him about that'n, Uncle Ather, he said. That'n you had.

Uncle Ather had already started. Oh yes, he said, allaying doubt with an upthrust of his chin. Yes, they

was, long time back. When I was a young feller, workin
on the road crew at that time, I caught one.

Caught one?

Yep. He smiled mysteriously. Shore did. Caught him
with my bare hands, and I got the scars to prove it.
Here he extended a leathery thumb for inspection. The
boy slid from his chair and bent studiously over it.

Right here, the old man said, pointing to a place on
the inside just above the web. See?

Yes, he said. The skin was wrinkled like an old purse;
in that myriad cross-hatching any line could have been
a scar. He sat back down and the old man chuckled
throatily.

Yessir, he said. He was a vicious critter. Must of
weighed all of five pound.

Warn laughed softly. The boy raised his head. The
old man sat complacent and mischievous in his rocker,
his eyes dancing.

Well, he said, this is what happent. They was a place
called Goose Gap—it's up t'wards Wears Valley. Well,
it was when we was blastin in there. Bill Munroe, he's
dead now, he went up right after, soon as rock quit
fallin, and then he hollered for me to come up and look
see. They's stit lots of smoke and dust and I couldn't
see too good but I got on up a little ways and directly
I seen he's holdin up somethin. Looked like a groundhog
or a little old dog. When I got to where he was at I
seen what it was. I hadn't never seen one afore and it
was all tore up and bloody, but I knowed right off what
it was. Bill, he couldn't make nothin out of it. What it
was was a painter kit.

We started up through them rocks and directly we
come up on anothern. It wadn't tore up as bad and Bill
allowed as to how it must not of been blowed as fer

and so we was headed right. Anyway it turned out he was right and in a little bit we come up on the den-hole. It was all blowed out in the front and about a yard and a half of bones layin all around, and back in the back under some rocks we found this'n, the third'n, he's alive and mewlin jest about like a housecat.

Old Bill, he backed off some, said that old she-painter might be around. Well, I was younger'n him and likely didn't have as good sense, so in I goes and grabs the little feller up by the scruff of the neck. That's when he hung his tushes in my thumb here. I turnt loose right fast, I'll tell ye. Well, I figured a minute, and then I took off my shirt and scotched him up in that and brought him on home with me.

Here the old man paused and helped himself to a chew of tobacco from a huge paper pouch. I lived five mile this side of Sevierville then, he continued. I—you boys don't chew, do ye? no—I had bought me a place off a man named Delozier—twenty acres, mostly side-hill and not much of a house neither, a old piece of a barn . . . I was married then and that was my first place so I reckon I was kindly what you might say proud of it. I kep some hogs and chickens and later on I had me a cow and a wore-out mule, put me in some corn . . . I never had nothin, ain't got nothin now, but I figured it was a start. I wadn't a whole lot older'n you fellers, nineteen, I think I was. But anyway what I was fixin to tell was about that painter. I brought him on home and give him to Ellen. She took to it right off, kep it in a box and give it milk and sech as that. It got to where it'd folly her around the house like a everday walkin-around cat. It wadn't but about the size of a cat too . . . I recollect he's speckled kindly like a bobcat. Well, they's even a feller come out from the newspaper and wrote it up about us havin him; folks come from pret-near everwhere to see him.

I reckon it was about two weeks we'd had him when one evenin I heard one of the hogs squeal. I got the lannern and went out but I couldn't find nothin wrong and went on back in and never thought no more about it. Well, next mornin they's a hog gone. I hadn't never heard of nobody stealin hogs but I figured maybe they's hog thieves jest like ary other kind, up in Sevier County leastwise as that was purty woolly country at that time. But they wadn't a whole lot I could do about it, not knowin where to even start lookin. Then two nights later anothern of em went. Well, I says, they gettin slicker now. The secont one never even squealt.

Next night I laid up on the roof of the house with the shotgun—a old single-barrel muzzleloader and me with not enough money to buy caps with even—I was usin matchheads and cottonseed hulls—and here's somebody stealin my hogs. So I laid up there all night, no further'n from here to the porch yonder from that hogpen. I never seed nothin nor heard nothin. Come mornin I never even looked at the hogs even. Then when she, Ellen, went out later on and slopped em she come back in and she says, Ather, they's another hog gone.

I was settin in a chair about half asleep and I come from there. I don't recollect how many hogs it was that we had but seven or eight I reckon anyway, and I run out and counted em and come up short one more hog. I'd been mad afore but now I was scared.

Here the old man found the cup of wine in his hand and he regarded it for a moment with mild surprise, raised it and took a drink. He closed his eyes for a moment,

the high wagon and them coming up to the house,

wagon and house both belonging to his uncle, and him owning nothing more than he could carry in his two hands, her things in an old leather trunk tied down behind the seat.

That her? he asked.

Yessir.

He walked around the wagon slowly, studying her as a man might a horse. Then he said, Well, light.

He got down and she was still sitting there.

What's she? goin to put the mule up?

Nosir, he said. Ellen. Here.

He took her hand and she got down.

You go on with Uncle Whitney, he said. I'll get the things.

Helen, he said.

It's Ellen, she said. The wagon moved away behind her.

Ellen.

Daddy said he'd kill him, she said.

Ain't nobody goin to kill nobody, he said. Here, watch the mud.

She said something else. He watched them go in.

What happent then, Uncle Ather, Warn said.

Hmm? Oh, well I'd done lost three of them I think it was then. That was three more'n I was willin to lose and two more'n I thought I would lose without I caught somebody. Aside that it looked like I would lose jest as many as whoever I was losin em to was willin to take, which probably meant all of them. So I was mad-scared. Ellen, she claimed I'd gone to sleep on the roof, but I knowed better.

That was late of a summer. I was stit on the road crew and workin twelve and fourteen hours a day and here I got to come home nights and set up with a bunch of hogs. But we never lost no more for a week or better. Then one night Ellen went to the door to thow out a pan of water and I heard her holler. I run out and she grabbed on to me like she'd seen a hant or somethin, and I ast her what it was but she jest stood there and shook like she's freezin to death. I walked her back in and went out and looked but I never seen nothin, so I got the pan and come on in. Somethin had scared her real bad but she couldn't tell me what all it was. After a while all she'd say was *I don't know*, or *I couldn't tell what it was.*

The old man paused again, arrested but for the rise and fall of his breathing, the slow mechanical rotation of his jaws, gazed upward—the image of the lampflame on the ceiling, the split corona a doubling egg, like the parthenogenesis of primal light.

He kept on for a week, coming back each night to the dark and empty house. Then he stopped going to work. That morning he took out the few things she had left—a housecoat, odds and ends, and put them on the bed. He sat and looked at them for a long time. When he got up it was evening.

He stayed for five more days, wandering about the house or sitting motionless, sleeping in chairs, eating whatever he happened to find until there wasn't any more and then not eating anything. While the chickens grew thin and the stock screamed for water, while the hogs perished to the last shoat. An outrageous stench settled over everything, a vile decay that hung in the air, filled the house.

On the sixth day he went out and knocked a plank from the back of the barn with the poll of his axe, cut from it two boards. On one he carefully incised her name with the point of his knife. Then he chopped a stake-point on the other board and nailed the two together in the form of a cross. He took it and took her clothes and a spade down to a corner of the lot where he scooped a hole, buried the clothes, and with the shank of the spade pounded the cross into the ground. Then he walked straight through the house and out again, across the yard, to the road and toward Sevierville. He had gone half a mile before he noticed the shovel in his hand and pitched it into the weeds.

I know you cain't, he said.

I ain't goin back.

I'll go out tomorrow. Come on, you clean up and eat some.

What?

And get some rest, sleep. I'll go out tomorrow.

Well, you can. I ain't.

I was goin out anyways. R. L. come by yesterday mornin to see if you was comin back. You goin back?

I don't know. No. I ain't goin back.

You aim to sell your place?

It don't . . . I don't care.

Well. I do.

He looked at him for the first time, the older face, dark and hard as a walnut. Why? he asked.

Count of you owe me two hunderd dollars, mainly.

Oh. He thought for a minute, then he said, Yes. Here, I got to clean up.

The old man was swaying slowly in his rocker holding the cup before him in both hands like a ciborium. After a minute Warn said, Did you ever find out what it was?

The old man turned and spat into a coffeecan.

That goddamned bibledrummer, wadn't it?

Don't say nothin else.

Well, nobody never died from it.

Don't say nothin else I told you.

Yessir, he said. It was the old she-painter, come after the little one. You boys care for some more wine?

They still had some. The old man labored up from his rocker and went to the table where he had set the wine, refilled his cup. Yep, he said, that had to of been what she seen.

Did you shoot it? the boy asked.

Nope. Never even seen her. I lost one more hog and then I give it up. I turnt the little one loose and that's the last I ever seen of it and the last hog I lost. You see, he said slowly, darkly, they's painters and they's painters. Some of em is jest that, and then others is right uncommon. That old she-painter, she never left a track one. She wadn't no common kind of painter.

Early next morning the old man worked his way up the mountain, following the prints of the two boys. The snow was drifted deeply in places and it was hard going. He stopped often to catch his breath, leaning on the shotgun, the stock sunk cleanly through the crust to the depth of the triggerguard. By the time he reached the road he was winded and leg-weary. From here he could see out into the valley, through the stark trees standing blackly in an ether of white like diffused milk, glazed and crystalline as shattered ice where the sun probed, the roofs thatched with snow, pale tendrils of smoke standing grayly in the still air.

He could smell smoke, but he didn't think about it until it occurred to him that it had a sharp and pungent quality about it and he realized that it was cedar burning—postwood, not firewood—elusive in the cold air, in his nostrils, faintly antiseptic.

He turned up the road and walked steadily until he

came to the cut-off to the pit. The snow was dry and powdered as marble-dust on his trouser legs. Now he could see the faint pall of smoke through the trees. The tracks turned here and furrowed in two drunken lanes, curving into the woods. He followed them, moving faster, stumbling in and out of the snow ruts, shadowed by some presentiment of ruin, into the clearing.

When he saw the smoke rolling up from out of the pit he stopped for a moment and he could feel the old fierce pull of blood in power and despair, the pulse-drum of the irrevocable act. And it was done, what soul rose in the ashes forever unknown, out of his hands now. He squatted on one knee in the snow, watching. On his face a suggestion of joy, of anguish—something primitive and half hidden. The pale eyes burned cold and remote in their hollows like pockets of smoldering gas.

He rose and retraced his steps back to the road. In the pit the amber coals glowed molten in their bed beneath the charred skeletons of the cedars.

Because the car was pulled over up the road and I couldn't see it from the creek. And he wadn't on the bridge when I come down but after I waded through and come out the other side he was standin on it lookin down at me and I seen him then and he said Come here.

So he took your traps.

All of em ceptin one, the boy said. He'd of had to of waded to find it so I never told him about it. He took the three of em. I didn't have but four.

Lowlife son of a bitch, Sylder said. What'd you tell him?

I never told him nothin. He said he was goin to take me to jail for trappin without license and bettin criminals. I told him I didn't know nothin bout some criminals.

Legwater, what'd he say?

Not much. Jest sort of grinned like a possum. Yeah, he said it'd go a lot easier on me if I was to tell em about it. That it was the same thing—bettin a criminal—as bein one your ownself. Then Gifford said that was right, how I'd likely get three to five years but that if I'd hep em out and tell who it was I might get off with jest a suspendered sentence.

But they didn't take you in?

No. He turned me loose at the forks, the store. He said soon as they got the rest of the evidence they'd pick me up and how it wouldn't do me no good to try to run.

He sat back in the chair, finished now and waiting to know what to do, just beginning to be not so scared.

Sylder leaned toward him. Listen, he said. You know that's all horseshit, don't you? You know what a ass it'd make him look to come draggin a fourteen-year-old boy in? Even for helpin a runner, let alone trappin without license? He's jest tryin to scare you. I know him. He cain't prove no way in the world you helped me and if they caught me it'd have to be with a load, in which case they wouldn't need nobody's testifyin, let alone yours, and even if they did I'd swear I never seen you before in my life and you'd do the same thing so they still couldn't bother you. It's all horseshit, tryin to bluff and scare you into helpin him poke his nose where it don't belong. He bothers you again you tell him nothin, tell him you'll get him for false arrest. Cept I don't think he's goin to bother you no more.

He said he'd catch you anyway.

He couldn't catch cowshit in a warshtub. It ain't even his business; he ain't the A. T. U. Anyway don't you let him bother you. I'll tend his apples for him my

ownself. He knowed you didn't have no daddy, nobody
to take up for you in the first place is the reason he
figured he could jump on you. He's a lowlife son of a
bitch and a caird to boot. Here, come take a look at
your pup; he's fat as a butterball. Come on, I got em on
the back porch on account of it bein so cold.

The pike had been cleared some time in the afternoon
so that he didn't even need the chains after he came off
the orchard road, dark now, something after six o'clock,
the rear end of the car heavy and swaying low over
the wheels even with the lovejoys set up as far as they
would go. It was very cold and his toes had not yet
thawed under the gas heater. He thought how the stump
of a toe in his left boot was particularly sensitive, remembering again *the sweep of the cutter's lights on the
stanchions of the bridge, the glazed and blinding eye
of the spotlight when it picked him out, standing on the
forward deck under a canopy of mangrove with his
foot braced on the cleat and holding the anchor rope.
When the light caught him he yelled once down into
the cabin and began hauling in on the rope. The starter
whirred and the motor coughed gutturally at the water,
the boat jostling, already moving. He got the anchor
in and watched the cutter lights. Even above the high
wheening of their own motor he could hear her revving
the big double Gray engines as she swung about, then
voices, commands, detached and sourceless on the steamy
calm of the Gulf. The cutter's spot followed them,
swamping them in light as they came out of the back-
water. He might have been a ballerina pirouetting there.
He could see the twin spume flaring from the prow of
the cutter, rising as she took speed, and the running
lights bobbing and bobbing again in the black wash of*

the cutwater. He heard the shots too, quite clearly, but made no association between them and himself. It didn't occur to him that he was being shot at until a real flurry broke out and he could see the muzzleflashes minute and intermittent like cigarettes glowing and hear the pebbly thoop thoop of the bullets in the passing water. Then he jumped and started for the cabin. Instantly there came the sounds of splintering wood and then something tore at his foot and threw him to the deck. He crawled to the companionway and slid down it on his belly.

Jimmy, he called, a hoarse whisper as if someone might hear them. Ho, Jimmy.

It was dark in the compartment except for the skittering glow of the searchlight passing and repassing the portholes, the portholes in bright silhouette wandering back and forth on the far wall.

Hey, kid. What you say?

Jimenez standing in the passageway. The tiller momentarily abandoned, the craft tilting full throttle across the water, the pulsing slap slap of it under the keel.

I'm shot, he said.

Jimenez holding the flashlight while he removed the shredded shoe, the sock sticky with blood, examined the pulpy mess of his big toe.

Where else, Mario?

I reckon that's it, he said.

Jimmy patting his shoulder commiseratingly. Is hard on the feets that, he said.

They went forward and he wrapped his toe in a strip torn from his shirt and sat there miserably, watching Jimenez's face green and serious in the glow of the panel lights.

He drove slowly, coming through the gap with the moon riding low over the pines that edged the long and barren slash of white beneath the power line, ice-fog coming up from the hollow, scintillant in the lights. Here where the inn stood, *the carnival atmosphere with the few cars strung alongside the road, the heat flicker-ing over them and the men standing about passing the last of the bottles back and forth, talking quietly now, their faces flushed and convivial. Some late arrivals claimed the blaze to have been visible from Vestal. Someone saying You done missed it, Marion.*

Was it a good'n?

Best you ever seen.

Nothin to be done there. A drink of whiskey, sneak-ing it now, Gifford having arrived. Gifford with a long pole poking steaming holes in the melt of glass. Gloop gloop. Vitreous tar. Damndest thing I ever seen. One brogan toe began to blister and blacken and a moment later he was hopping away snatching at his shoelaces. Goddamn. Whew. Leaning against a tree with his naked foot cradled in his hands like a hurt bird he dared a snicker with fierce eyes.

And two days later the charred shaft of the pine tree still smoldering, pitch bubbling gently from the shell of the bark and small electricblue flames seeping and curl-ing, the spire of smoke standing straight up in the mo-tionless air like a continuation of the tree itself.

On the curve below the gap the rear wheels drifted slightly and he realized that there was a thin sheet of ice on the road. He sat up over the wheel and wiped the glass with a rag. He passed Tipton's, the lights above the road warm and friendly-looking through the trees. Old married men. Sylder chuckled, reached for his cig-arettes. *He was the nicest boy . . . the rain peening steadily the tin roof of the church, obelisks of light slanting down from the high windows like buttresses. After the creak of the door nothing but the huge breath-*

ing silence, musty odor, the patient and quiet abandonment, chairs, benches, the pulpit, all orderly and still in their coats of dust, an air of mild surprise about them at this late visitation. Their steps ghostly on the warping boards, rousing an owl from the beams, passing over them on soundless wings, a shadow, ascending into the belfry like an ash sucked up a flue and as silently. She gripped his arm. Together to the mourners' bench. O Lord, O Lord. Witnessed by one nightbird.

Topping the hill above the creek he came upon a half-ton truck with a horse on it, the long bland face peering down at him over the slatted tailgate with eyes luminous and round as bottlebottoms in the carlights. The truck was laboring at the hill with beetle-like industry, the gears grinding out a low whine. He watched the snow swirling over the road behind it, serpentine, white wisps like smoke on glass, eased up the shiftlever and passed them, the horse's off eye rolling wildly, past the cab, the driver dimly lit within, puffing at a cigar, looking down at him once.

One side for the hooch man, Sylder said. New Year's whiskey comin. Figure ten headaches to the gallon, makes . . . a thousand . . . about twelve hunderd real hat stretchers. How about that, old man?

Old man puffed his cigar, receding rearward, dimmed his lights to one dull orange globe.

He drove straight down Gay Street, halting obediently at the stoplights, gazing at the numbed traffic officers with insolent bemusement.

Howdy, Blue-boy. Keer for a drink?

Out on the west side of town he pulled into a drive and around behind an aged and ill-kept frame house. He backed the coupe up to the garage and got out, stretching a little. Two men came from the house, the kitchen, where a small window was lit. Another man came to the door and stood there leaning against the jamb, his shirttail out, smoking a cigarette and taking the air. A woman's voice small and shrill somewhere in the house behind him: Shet the door, idjit. You raised in a barn? He didn't move.

Howdy, Sylder, the first man said, going past him to the garage, not even looking at him.

Howdy, Sylder said.

The other one stopped. How's the new car? he asked.

All right.

Ward says it come out of Cosby.

Could be.

Ward says it's plenty fast. Says they blockaded the feller on the Newport highway is the only way they ever come to catch him at all.

Let's go, Tiny, the other man called from the garage.

Sylder went to the rear of the coupe and opened the decklid. They began to unload, carrying the cases back into the garage, the car creaking and rising bit by bit until they had finished and it stood with its rear end high in the air like a cat in heat.

Sylder took a flashlight and wrench from the glove compartment, stooped by the rear wheels each in turn and lowered the car. Then he undid the chains, got in and drove off them, came back and put them in the trunk. The motor was still running and as he slid behind the wheel once more Tiny came to lean on the door.

Don't she sound sweet though, he said.

Sylder looked up at him. That what Ward says?

Tiny grinned. Naw, he said. Seems to me that's what McCrary said. When Ward loant him the money to buy it.

Tell Ward good cars costs good money. Even at a government auction. Or even if you done paid for em oncet.

He set the gears and ran the motor up once and Tiny stood up. Come back, he said.

Sylder was rolling up the glass. We'll see ye, he said, switched on the headlights and pulled away down the drive.

He drove slowly back to the mountain, past the forks and the store, the porch posts dead-white as plaster casts of those untrimmed poles, the huge carved lion's head in fierce cameo upon the door, the brass knocker brightly pendant from its nostrils, and the barred panes buckling in the light planeless as falling water, passing out of the glare in willowing sheets to darkness, stark and stable once again. Past his own house, dark but for the light on the porch, and then across the mountain, still slowly, pulling the grades down under the wheels easily.

The road was glazed with ice on the far side and he amused himself by drifting the coupe from curve to curve like a boat tacking. At the foot of the mountain he left Henderson Valley Road and turned right down Bay's Mountain Road, driving on gravel now, slowing to some ten or fifteen miles an hour and finally switching off the headlights. He drove that way for half a mile, the coupe rolling ghostly over the road, black and silent against the snow. Then he turned the car around in a drive, pointing it back down the road, and got out.

He walked up the road until he came to the next drive and here he turned in, plodding through the snow to the lightless house where it brooded in a copse of trees, solitary above the empty fields, over and around it the naked branches tangled like ironwork.

He walked around the house twice. No dogs barked. At the back again he tested a window, lifted it, the weights slithering in the sashes, stepped through and inside. He found himself in an areaway off the kitchen, two doors in front of him, one leading to a large open room, the other one closed.

Hola, Jeffo, he called, whispered, in mock and inaudible greeting. *Dorme?* On downpointed cat's feet he stepped the three steps to the closed door and folded his hand over the knob. Oh, Jeffo, he whispered. *Es muy malo que no tengas un perro.* Turned the knob and opened the door.

There was one small high window in the room, a square of gray standing out of the blackness, and other than that he could see nothing. He stood at the door for a few minutes, listening to the rumbling breath of the man asleep. After a while he could make out the shape of the bed, directly in front of him.

It was warm in the room, he could feel the sweat in his armpits, but the man was swathed heavily in blankets. Thickness of them under his hand . . . here shape of arm, of shoulder, chest . . . sleeping on his back. Gifford snuffled. One gluey eyelid came unstuck as the covers receded from his chin with maternal solicitude.

He even raised his head a little, wonderingly, sleep leaving him in slow grudging waves, so that he seemed to be coming up to meet it, the shut fist rocketing down out of blackness and into his face with a pulpy sound like a thrown melon bursting.

When he got home it was past midnight and had turned off colder yet. He parked the coupe at the back of the house, scotched the wheel and went in through the kitchen. He took some biscuits and a jar of preserves from the icebox and ate them, walking up and down a little, flexing his knuckles. When he had finished he put the preserves back, took a long drink from a jar of buttermilk, and then went into the bedroom. His right hand was swollen and he picked delicately at the buttons of his coat.

Marion . . .?

Yeah, he said.

Oh . . . what time is it?

Late, I reckon. I got tied up.

Are you okay?

Yeah.

He stepped out of his trousers and crawled in beside her.

She could feel him laughing silently. What? she said.

He kept astin who it was.

What? Who did.

Hmm? Naw, nothin. Just some feller. Go on to sleep.

She turned over and put her hand on his chest. She said, Hush.

He lay on his back, his hand over hers, the other hand stiffening. Suddenly he had a bile-sharp foretaste of disaster. *Why was that old man shooting holes in the government tank on the mountain?*

You sure have got cold feet, she said.

He stared up at the dark ceiling. *I'll be damned if I do,* he whispered to himself.

IV

A warm wind on the mountain and the sky darkening, the clouds looping black underbellies until a huge ulcer folded out of the mass and a crack like the earth's core rending rattled panes from Winkle Hollow to Bay's Mountain. And the wind rising and gone colder until the trees bent as if borne forward on some violent acceleration of the earth's turning and then that too ceased and with a clatter and hiss out of the still air a plague of ice.

The old man looked out through a veil of water fringing his hatbrim, beadwork swinging as he turned his head. The hail had stopped and the wind was coming up again with the rain. He had set forth from his refuge under the claybank and already he was wet through. The road had gone from dust shocked up in dark waterballs to geysers of erupting mud, a sluggish flow beginning in the wheelruts and blistering under the rain. The old man began to run, hobbling in an odd bandylegged progress through the blinding rain, great windblown sheets of it sweeping over the road. The air was filled with branches and foliage of trees and the trees whipped and cracked. By the time he left the road and entered the woods they were coming down, the dead and leafless trunks, grasping with brittle gray fingers and going prone on the earth with the muffled thunder of their fall half lost in the fulminations overhead. The old man kept to his course, over last year's leaves slick with water, hopping and dancing wildly among the maelstrom of riotous greenery like some rain sprite, burned out of the near-darkness in antic configuration against the quick bloom of the lightning. As he passed it thus a barren chestnut silver under the sluice of rain erupted to the heart and spewed out sawdust and scorched mice upon him. A slab fell away with a long hiss like a burning mast tilting seaward. He is down. A clash of shields rings and Valkyrie descend with cat's cries to bear him away. Already a rivulet is packing clay in one ragged cuff and a quiff of white hair depending from his forelock reddens in the seeping mud.

Rainwater seeped among the porous boards of the outhouse until the windrowed leaves in the cat's corner were black and lifeless and the cat left through the leaning door to seek new shelter. Pools of black water stood in the path swirling slowly their wrack of straw and weeds, armadillo beetles coiled round as shot and strangely buoyant. She skirted them on wincing feet, bore squeamishly the wet slide of last year's limp and slimebrown weeds.

Arthur Ownby's hound rooted and burrowed in his wad of ripe sacks, slept again, his tail clasped to his hairless stomach. He did not see the cat that came to the door of his cellar and stood on three legs.

Such light as there was to announce the new day filtered thinly through a mizzle of rain and remarked the fluff of her taupe fur curled in a cleft treebole on the south slope of Red Mountain. Hunger drove her out in the late afternoon, cautious, furtive, dusted with wood-rot.

Still the rain, eating at the roads, cutting gullies on the hills till they ran red and livid as open wounds. The creek came up into the fields, a river of mud questing among the honeysuckles. Fenceposts like the soldiers of Pharaoh marched from sight into the flooded draws.

In Saunders' field a shallow marsh, calm and tractable beneath the dimpling rain. And yet rain. What low place did not hold water? At the little end of McCall's pond water fell thunderously into the sinkhole that drained it. Along Little River the flats stood weed-deep in livercolored water flecked with thatches of small driftwood and foam that coiled and spun near imperceptibly, or rocked with the wind-riffles passing under them. By day flocks of rails gathered. A pair of bitterns stalked with gimlet eyes the fertile shallows. At night the tidelands rang with peepers, with frogs gruffly choral. Great scaly gars from the river invaded the flats, fierce and primitive of aspect, long beaks full of teeth, ancient fishes survived unchanged from mesozoic fens, their yellowed boneless skeletons graced the cracked clay-beds later in the season where the water left them to what querulous harridans, fishcrow or buzzard, might come to glean their frames, the smelly marvel of small boys.

Rafts of leaves descended the flowage of Henderson Valley Road, clear water wrinkling over the black asphalt. The mud-choked gullies ran thick with water of a violent red, roiling heavily, pounding in the gutters with great belching sounds. The cat trod the high crown of the road, bedraggled and diminutive, a hunted look about her.

A low sun fired the pine knots in the smokehouse wall till they glowed like rubies, veined and pupiled eyes, peering in at the gloom where the cat gnawed a dangling side of pork-ribs. The salt drew her mouth but she kept at it, pausing now and again to listen at the silence. Mildred Rattner's mule-slippers carried her with care past the bad spots in the mud, chancing rather the dampness of the ragged grass that grew along the path. What with the pat of rain on the tarpaper overhead the cat heard nothing until the keys jangled just beyond the door and the lock rattled. She leapt to a high shelf, poised, sprang again, making for the air vent under the peaked roof. As the door let in she was hanging by one toenail from this opening, hindclaws flailing desperately for purchase, and then a sliver of the molding wood gave way and she lost her grip.

When Mildred Rattner swung open the door and stepped into the smokehouse she saw a cat drop with an anguished squall from somewhere overhead, land spraddle-legged facing her, and make a wild lunge at her, teeth gleaming in the dimness and eyes incandesced with madness. She screamed and fell backwards and the cat with a long despairing wail flowed over her and was gone.

In Tipton's field four crows sat in a black locust, ranged upon the barren limbs with heads low between their wingblades, surveying the silvergray desolation, the silent rain in the country. They watched the cat come

across the field at a slow lope, an erratic dancing progress where she veered and leapt, keeping to the spotty
dry ground. Their calls in the afternoon stillness had
a somber loneliness about them, the mournful quality
of freight whistles. They came from the roost and de-
filed low over her head, dipping and swooping. The cat
spun low on her haunches, batted at them. So did they
harry her out of the field, her pausing at each attack to
make a stand and grapple at the wind of their passage,
hard-pressed to preserve dignity, the birds flaring, wheeling, setting to again in high crude humor. They left her
at the bank of the creek to return, settle with treading
wings among the locust branches. She marked them
down, her yellow eyes narrowed in contempt, turned
downstream and followed the swollen creek to the
bridge. Here she crossed and continued, taking the high
wooded ground on the south bank, pausing here and
there with random inquisitiveness at holes and hollow
logs to smell, shake herself or lick the water from her
chest, until a strong odor of mink musk brought her
to the creek proper again.

The mink was dead, swaying in the shore currents
among the swamped and flaring grass. She crept to it on
cocked legs, leapt to a mud hummock and swatted it
with a long reach downward. She stood up and watched
it. It bobbed lifelessly. The chain was hung on a stob
somewhere out in the water and when she hooked her
claws into the mink to pull it toward her it did not
come. Finally she ventured one foot into the water and
bit into the neck of the animal. The grit impregnated
in its fur set her teeth on edge and she attacked it sav-
agely, then stopped suddenly as if her attention had
wandered or returned to something of importance which
she had forgotten. She left the mink and set a course
across the fields toward the pike road.

The rain had plastered down her fur and she looked very thin and forlorn. She gathered burdock and the curling purple leaves of rabbit weed as she went; a dead stalk of blackberry briar clung to her hind leg. Just short of the road she stopped, shivered her loose skin, ears flat against her head. She squalled once, hugging the ground with her belly, eyes turned upward at the colorless sky, the endless pelting rain.

On the afternoon of the third day the rain slacked and through the high pall of faint gray, blades of light swung like far beacons, cutting slowly the wisped cloud edges, lace-tatter or swirl of sea mist. Dark fell early, and later as he lay quilted and awake in his black loft the rainless silence of the roof seemed to measure time, something lying in wait. He had already decided to go to the creek in the morning. The water might even have fallen some.

So it was the morning of the fourth day before he went to his traps again, passing the pond and skirting the lower end where it flared out into the field with the weeds standing in the water like rice, then down along the limestone ledges, past the hail-shattered floats of water lilies, shoals of new green leaves, on across the field and out to the road.

Before he came to the bridge he left the road, turned down a steep bank and crossed a fence, following a mud path until he came out on the creek bank. It had not fallen any. Troughs of clayey water rocked through the shallow field on the far side, seething in the matted honeysuckle, the tops of milkweeds and willow shoots quivering in the pull of it. The creek itself was a roily misshapen flume more like solid earth in motion than any liquid, cutting past him, each dip and riffle, eddy, glide, uncurling rope coil fixed and changeless and only the slight oily tremor of the water and the rush of noise testifying to motion at all. Unless a limb or stick came down, or here: a fluted belt of water curling upward in a long scoop like a snarled lip broken suddenly by a tree branch lashing out of the perfect opacity of it, rapid and deft as a snake striking, subsiding again and invisible with no ring or ripple to trace it by. He sat down for a few minutes and watched it all. A kingfisher came up the creek, tacking back and forth, saw the boy and flared, veered away over the watery fields trailing in the morning quiet his high staccato call.

He got up and started along the path over the shelf of woods between the creek and the mountain, by hickories feathered in mist, by cottonwoods still coldly skeletal for all the new green of the spring. He began to climb, his approach forewarned by the patter of nut hulls, a dipping branch, scrabble of small feet on bark. He crossed the spine of the ridge and started down, seeing the horseshoe bend of the creek below him distended with blisters of brown water spread out into the fields, down the slope to the creek again—a shortcut he took, who measured only horizontal travel.

He couldn't find it. The creek was none that he had ever seen before, and when he turned his back to it at what looked like a place he knew he was surprised to see a draw, a fence-corner, a stand of locust oddly mis-located. He passed the place and came back. He had been too far down. He hurried along upstream for another fifty yards and then stopped short. The rock where his trap had been was submerged, but a dome of water rose over it and now he saw the wire reaching up to the sapling on the opposite bank. Just above here the creek narrowed—it was the place where he usually crossed on a long and mossy pier of stone, that too lost now beneath the floodwaters. In the narrows the current leaped in a slick chute, plummeted into the pool below, churning a chocolate-dark foam and spreading again, a hissing sheet of flecks and bubbles, small twigs, bark and debris. A naked and swollen young bird turned up its round white belly briefly, rolled and folded into the thick brown liquid like a slowly closing eye. And below the rock something roiled darkly to the surface, sank again, as if struggling with some unseen assailant. He watched. A moment later it flared again and he could make it out better, the hair floating undulant as black grass wracked in the eddies. He looked along the bank until he found a stick, came back and leaned on tiptoes out over the water, poking. He found the ledge of rock, tested along it with his stick and then stepped out, panicky for a moment as his foot sank. Then he was straddle-legged with one foot on the bank and the other in the creek, the water boiling between his legs, ribboning high on his calf. He got the other foot down and turned, carefully, facing upstream, standing with the thin brown wings of water flying over his shins with a slicing sound, standing so in an illusion of fantastic motion. He worked his way crabwise to within a yard of the other bank, to the channel where the rocks terminated, launched out wildly across the remaining stretch of water. He went in nearly to his waist, his feet chopping rapidly at the slick and steep-pitched mud, flailing mightily with his stick before he could get a proper foothold. Then he was across, pulling himself up the bank by what roots or weeds would hold his weight, cold and mud-slavered.

He hobbled down to where the sapling was and slid down the bank to it, catching himself with one foot against the slender trunk, took hold of the wire and undid it, the wire humming electrically in his hand, took a good grip on it and climbed the bank again pulling

it after him. When he got to the top and turned around
he could see his catch floating in the grass and even before he pulled it up to him he could see the white places
on it like hanging leeches. Then he had it in his hand,
feeling the fur gritty with mud, the cusped bone-end
jutting from the foreleg wrecked between the jaws of
the trap, the white bib smeared with clay and the fine
yellow teeth bared in a fierce grin. And turning it slowly
in his hand, studying dumbly the clean ugly slits, white
and livid. Wounds, but like naked eyelids or dead
mouths gaping.

He took it from the trap and put it in his pocket,
wound the wire around the trap and put that in the
other pocket. The sun was well up, but already the
promised light was drowned in a sweep of wet clouds
rolling and building darkly to the southeast. He did
not recross the creek but headed out into the field. Before he reached the woods the first drops of rain had
already spattered his shoulder. When he got to the road
it was black and slick with water and he hunched his
shoulders forward against the mounting downpour, shivering a little. Sheets of spray gusted over the smoking
road and over the swamped land—the houses standing
bleak and gray—a final desolation seemed to come, as
if on the tail of the earth's last winter a well of water
were rising slowly up through the very universe itself.

It had been raining for six days steady when Marion
Sylder finally left the house. He came down the drive
sideways, slewing sheets of mud from under the cavort-
ing wheels, got straightened out on the road and drove
to the forks. A small pond had formed in front of the
store and customers were obliged to tread a plankwalk
to get to the porch. The rain had settled into a patient drizzle and the people of Red Branch sat around

their stoves, looked out from time to time at the gray wet country and shook their heads. Sylder backed his car up to the gas pump and got out, sloshing the mud from his boots in the puddle, waded to the porch and went in. There was a mesh of welding rod over the front windows now and he smiled a little at that.

Mr Eller looked up from his chair by the meat block. Well, he said, ain't seen you for a while. Bring some money with ye?

Sylder ignored that. Gas, he said. Where's the keys?

Mr Eller sighed and rose from his chair, went to the cash register, rang open the drawer, handed the keys across the counter.

Hope you don't keer to wade, he said.

Sylder took the keys and went out to the pump. He unlocked it and began cranking the lever, pumping gas up into the glass bowl at the top of the rusty orange tank. When he had it full he unscrewed the cap from the fender, let in the hose and depressed the lever. The gas in the bowl surged and bubbled, sluiced into the tank of the car. After the bowl emptied it remained beaded on the inside, a greasy look to it. Sylder didn't notice. He re-hung the hose and locked the pump, waded back to the porch and inside to give the keys to Mr Eller. A loosed box of kittens came tottering aimlessly over the floor, rocking on their stub legs and mewling. Their eyes were closed and festered with mucus as if they might have been struck simultaneously with some biblical blight.

Them's the nastiest-lookin cats I ever did see, Sylder said.

That's what Mrs Fenner said, droned the storekeeper. Young Pulliam told her she ought to see the ones back in the back propped up with sticks. He picked the keys up off the counter and rang them back in the cash drawer again.

Put it on the bill, Sylder said.

Seems like they ought to be a handsign for that, Mr Eller said. Like for Howdy or we'll see ye. Save a lot of talk in here.

If I had your money I'd retire for life.

It'd pay about the same.

Sure it would, Sylder said.

Seems to me like, Mr Eller began . . .

Never mind, Sylder said. I got to get on. Poor folks don't have time to stand around jawin all day.

He waved and went out, stopped at the door a minute and looked back. Say, he called.

What's that?

A Christian'd of drownded em.

What's that? Mr Eller asked again.

Leaning in the door and grinning Sylder pointed at the kittens bobbing over the floor like blown lint.

Mr Eller shooed his hand at him and he left.

The storekeeper drummed his nails on the marble ledge of the cash register for a minute. Then he turned and went back to his chair. He had been resting for only a short time when the clock among the canned goods began a laborious unwinding sound as if about to expire violently in a jangle of wheels and leaping springs, stopped, tolled off four doomlike gongs evocative of some oriental call to temple, then hushed altogether.

Mr Eller stirred from his chair, went to the clock and wound it with a key hanging down from a string. It made a loud ratcheting noise. Then he seized it from the shelf and slammed it back. It set up once more a low wooden ticking.

One of the cats had wandered behind the meat block and on his return to the chair he stepped over it carefully. It went by in a drunken reel, caromed off the meat case, continued. Lost, they wandered about the floor, passing and repassing each other, unseeing. One staggered past a coffecan set next the stove, slipped, fell in the puddle of tobacco spittle surrounding it. He struggled to his feet again, back and side brown-slimed and sticky, tottered across to the wall where he stood with blind and suppurant eyes and offered up to the world his thin wails.

Mr Eller dozed and his head rocked in small increments down his shoulder, onto his chest. After a while a little girl in a thin and dirty dress came through the door behind the counter and gathered up all the kittens, now wailing louder and in broken chorus, carried them out again, talking to them in low remonstrances.

Mr Eller dozed, the clock ticked. The flypaper revolved in slow spirals. The wind had come up again and the rainwater blown from the trees pattered across the tin roof of the store, muffled and distant-sounding through the wallboard ceiling.

Sylder closed the gate behind him and started up the orchard road. It was guttered and channeled and sluices of water still seeped along the myriad mud deltas that filled the flats between the inclines. The car slewed giddily on the turns, bogged finally to a frantic stop skittering quarterwise like a nervous horse and the rear wheels unwinding thick ropes of mud that broke and shot precipitately across the low hem of brush and on into the woods where they slapped up against the trees with a sound oddly hollow. Sylder cut the motor and stepped out into the bright mud. It was a quarter mile to the turnaround and he started straightaway, his leather boots sucking.

There were apples on the trees the size of a thumb-nail and green with a lucent and fiery green, deathly

green as the bellies of bottleflies. He plucked one down
in passing and bit into it . . . venomously bitter, drew
his mouth like a persimmon. If green apples made you
sick, Sylder reflected, he would have been dead long
ago. Most people he knew could eat them. Didn't take
poison ivy either. The boy John Wesley, he was bad
about poison ivy. Bad blood.

It took him until dark to get done, joggling the cases
two at a time back down the road, nine trips in all.
When he had stacked the last two cases in the turtle
he locked it and opening the door of the car sat down
and took off his boots, shapeless with mud, and stood
them on the floor just behind the front seat.

He got the car rocked loose and then had to back
down for almost half a mile before he could find a place
that looked wide and solid enough to turn around in.
By the time he got out on the pike a wind had come up
and small spits of rain were breaking on the glass. He
propped his left sock foot on the handbrake and drove
leisurely down the mountain.

The lights of the city hovered in a nimbus and again
stood fractured in the black river, isinglass image, tangled
broken shapes: the shapeless splash of lights along the
bridgewalk following the elliptic and receding rows of
pole lamps across to meet them. The rhythmic arc of
the wipers on the glass lulled him and he coasted out
onto the bridge, into the city shrouded in rain and
silence, the cars passing him slowly, their headlamps
wan, watery lights in sorrowful progression.

Sylder's motor spat and jerked, caught again for a
handful of revolutions, died with a spastic sucking noise.
He let in the clutch and coasted for a minute, engaged it
again. The motor bucked and the car shuddered violently and came to a stop.

He sat at the wheel of the motionless car for a minute

or two before he tried the starter. It cranked cheerfully, caught and sputtered once or twice without ever running. He flipped the switch off, reached a flashlight from the glove compartment, took a deep breath and surged wildly out into the rain. Waist-deep in the engine compartment with the upturned hood sheltering him like the maw of some benevolent monster he checked the wiring, the throttle linkages. Then he removed the float-bowl from the fuel pump, held the flashlight up to the glass and looked at it. The liquid in it was a pale yellow. He poured it out and replaced the bowl, dropped the hood and got back in the car. He had to crank the engine for some time before the bowl filled again and then the motor caught and he engaged the gears. He drove along cautiously, listening. The streetlamps passed bleary whorls along the window; there was no more traffic. Before he got to the end of the bridge the motor rattled and died again.

The old man awoke to darkness and water running, trickling and coursing beneath the leaves, and the rain very soft and very steady. The hound was lying with its head on crossed forepaws watching him. He reached out one hand and touched it and the dog rose clumsily and sniffed at his hand.

The wind had died and the night woods in their faintly breathing quietude held no sound but the kind rainfall, track of waterbeads on a branch—their measured fall in a leaf-pool. With grass in his mouth the old man sat up and peered about him, heard the rain mendicant-voiced, soft chanting in that dark gramarye that summons the earth to bridehood.

They came three times for the old man. At first it was just the Sheriff and Gifford. They were one foot up the porch steps when he swung the door open and threw down on them and they could see the mule ears of the old shotgun laid back viciously along the locks. They turned and went back down the yard, not saying anything or even looking back, and the old man closed the door behind them.

The second time they pulled up in the curve of the road with three deputies and a county officer. The old man watched them from his window darting and skulking among the bushes, slipping from tree to tree like boys playing Indians. After a while when everyone was set the Sheriff called from his place under the bank of the road.

Come out with your hands up, Ownby. We got you surrounded.

The old man never even turned his head. He was in the kitchen with the shotgun propped over the back of the chair and he was watching one of the deputies hunkered up under a lilac bush in the west corner of the lot. The old man kept watching him and then the Sheriff called out again for him to surrender and somebody shot out a window-glass in the front room so he didn't wait any more but pulled the stock in against his cheek and cut down on the deputy. The man came up out of the bushes like a rabbit and hopped away toward the road with a curious loping gait, holding the side of his leg. He'd expected the man to yell and he didn't, but then the old man remembered that he hadn't yelled either.

The kitchen glass exploded in on him then and he got behind the stove. There was a cannonade of shots from the woods and he sat there on the floor listening to it and to the spat spat of the bullets passing through the house. Little blooms of yellow wood kept popping out on the planks and almost simultaneously would be the sound of the bullet in the boards on the other side of the room. They did not whine as they passed through. The old man sat very still on the floor. One shot struck the stove behind him and leaped off with an angry spang, taking the glass out of the table lamp. It was like being in a room full of invisible and malevolent spirits.

He had the shotgun across his knees, broken, still holding the empty shell in his hand. The firing died in a few minutes and he crawled along the cupboard and got his shells off the table and came back and reloaded the empty chamber. Then he rolled a cigarette. He could hear them calling to one another. Someone wanted to know if anyone was hurt. Then the Sheriff told them to hold up a minute, that the old bastard hadn't shot since the first time, and hollered loud, as if a person couldn't hear him anyway, wanting to know if Ownby was ready to come out now.

The old man lit his cigarette and took a deep pull. Outside all was silence.

Ownby, the Sheriff called, come out if you're able.

There was more silence and finally he heard some voices and after that they fired a few more rounds. The stick propping up the glassless window leaped out on the floor and the window dropped shut. He could hear the bits of lead hopping about in the front room, chopping up the furniture and scuttling off through the walls and rafters like vermin.

They stopped and the Sheriff was talking again. Spread out, he was saying. Keep under cover as much as you can and remember, everybody goes together.

That didn't make much sense to the old man. He pulled twice more on his cigarette and put it out and crawled under the stove. Through a split board he could see them coming, looking squat above the grass from his low position. Two deputies were moving down from the south end with drawn pistols. One of them was dressed in khakis and looked like an A T U agent. The old man marked their position, wiggled back out from under the stove, riposted to the window and shot them both in quick succession, aiming low. Then he ducked back to his stove, broke the shotgun, extracted the shells and reloaded. No sound from outside. The Sheriff did not call again and after a while when he heard the cars starting he got up and went to the front room to see what they'd shot up.

Toward late afternoon it began to rain again but the old man couldn't wait any longer. Black clouds were moving over the mountain, shading the sharp green of it, and in the coombs horsetails of mist clung or lifted under the wind to lace and curl wistfully, break and trail across the lower slopes. A yellowhammer crossed the yard to his high hole in the jagged top of a lightning-wrecked pine, under-wings dipping bright chrome.

The old man carried out the last of his things and piled them on the sledge, buckled them down with the harness straps he had nailed under the sides. He went back in one more time and looked around. Some last thing he could save. He came out at length with a small hooked rug, shook the dust from it and put it over the top of the sledge. He took up the rope and pulled the sledge to the road and called for Scout. The old dog came from under the porch, peering with blue rheumy eyes at his indistinct world of shapes. The old man called again and the dog started for the road, hobbling stiffly, and they set out together, south along the road, until they were faint and pale shapes in the rain.

So when they came for the old man the third time he was not there. They lobbed teargas bombs through the windows and stormed the ruined house from three sides and the house jerked and quivered visibly under their gunfire. A county officer was wounded in the neck. He sat on the muddy ground with the blood running down his shirtfront, crying, and calling out to the others to Get the dirty son of a bitch. When they came back out of the house no one would look at him. Finally the Sheriff and another man came to where he was and helped him up and took him to the car.

No, the Sheriff said. He got away.

Got away? How could he get away. The man asked two or three times but the Sheriff just shook his head and after that the man didn't ask any more. They left in a spray of mud, four cars of them, with sirens going.

. . .

When the old man came out upon the railroad the rain had moved off the mountain and in the last light under the brim of the clouds he could see the long sharp ridges like lean burning hounds racing down the land to the land's end westward, hard upon the veering sun. He turned his back to them, going east on the railbed, the sledge rocking over the moldering ties. It was still raining and dark was coming on fast. From time to time he stopped to check his load and cinch the harness straps up. For two hours he followed the tracks, down out of the darkening fields through cuts where night fell on the high banks and fell upon the honeysuckle drawing shadow forms there, grotesques, shapes of creatures mythical or extinct and silently noting his passage. The old man bent east along the tracks, leaning into the rope, into the rich purple dusk.

By full dark he had left the tracks and turned into the woods to the south, feeling out the path with his feet, shivering a little now in his wet clothes. They came past the old quarry, the tiered and graceless monoliths of rock alienated up out of the earth and blasted into ponderous symmetry, leaning, their fluted faces pale and recumbent among the trees, like old temple ruins. They went silently along over the trace of the quarry road, the sledge whispering, the gaunt dog padding, past the quarryhole with its vaporous green waters and into the woods again, the limestone white against the dark earth, a populace of monstrous slugs dormant in a carbon forest. Groups of trees turned slowly like masted carousels, blending shadows and parting in darkness and wonder. The rain stopped falling. They passed, leaving a trail of foxfire shuffled up out of the wet leaves like stars plowed in a ship's wake.

Morning found them on the south slope of Chilhowee

Mountain, the dog buckled down on top of the sledge now and the old man pulling them tree by tree up the steep and final rise. From his high place on the slope he could see the first strawcolored light sourceless beyond the earth's curve, the horizon warped in a glaucous haze. An hour later and they had gained the crest of the mountain and stood in a field of broom sedge bright as wheat, treeless but for a broken chestnut the color of stone.

The sun was up by then and the old man rested, leaning against the tree. After a while he fell asleep, the sledge's painter still wrapped in his blistered hand. The dog stretched out in the sun too, wrinkling his ragged hide at the flies. Far below them shades of cloud moved up the valley floor like water flowing, darkened the quilted purlieus, moved on, the brushed land gone green and umber once again. The clouds broke against the mountain, coral-edged and bent to the blue curve of the sky. A butterfly struggled, down through shells of light, down to the gold and seagreen tree tips . . .

The old man came awake late in the afternoon and ate some cold cornbread, sharing it with the hound. He did not eat much and the cornbread was enough. Then he started down the mountain, trucking behind him his sorry chattel, picking a course through the small trees and laurel jungles. Some time after midnight he came out on a road and turned south along it, crossed a wooden bridge, a purling clearwater stream, climbed with the road into the mountains again, the sledge drifting easily behind him and the hound plodding.

The light at the house the old man came to that morning he could see a good while before he got to it. He caught glimpses of it once or twice somewhere on the ridge above him as he was coming through a mountain meadow, a huge pool in the darkness swept with the passing shadows of nightbirds, but he had no way of knowing that the road would take him there. He didn't see the light again until he topped the hill where the house stood and where a section of road was banded out of the night in a tunnel of carlights. Some men were talking and he could hear the sound of the motor running.

He kept on, into the light. The voices stopped. The old man looked up at them, two men leaning against the side of the automobile, another seated inside. He didn't stop. They faded behind the glare of the headlights, reappeared filmily, not moving, watching him. With the lights out of his eyes the old man stopped and nodded to them. Howdy, he said.

You ain't lost, are ye?

Don't reckon, he said.

One of them said something. The car eased down the drive, the two men walking alongside. The man in the car leaned out toward him. This road don't go thew, he said. It jest loops and comes on back.

How fer is it to the Harrykin? the old man wanted to know.

The man turned out the lights. The other two had come up now and said Howdy, each in turn. Scout clambered up onto the sledge and eyed them balefully.

Wants to know how fer is it to the Harrykin, the driver said.

What fer?

The other one stepped forward and eyed the old man with bland curiosity, the sledge heaped with his worthless paraphernalia and topped by the prone and wasted hound. You cain't hardly get there from here, he said. You ort to of come thew Sunshine, crost the river there . . . it ain't easy to get to from nowhere but that-there'd of been a nigher cut. What you aim to do in there, cut timber?

No, said the old man. Jest fixin to put up some kind of a piece of a house and kindly settle there.

In the Harrykin?

Yessir.

Where-all you from? the man in the car wanted to know.

From t'wards Knoxville.

The man in the car was silent for a minute. Then he said, I'm goin in to Sevierville here in jest a minute. I can carry you that fer if you don't keer to ride in a old beat-up car such as it is.

Much obliged, the old man said, but I reckon I'll jest get on.

Well, the man said. He turned to the other two. I got to get, myself, he said. We'll see yins.

They nodded. You come back. The car eased away, the lights coming on again, rattled out of sight down the road. The old man had the sledge rope in hand and was saying a goodbye to the men.

You best come on in and have some breakfast with us, one of them said.

Much obliged, the old man said, but I reckon I'll jest be gettin on.

Might as well eat some with us, the other said. We jest fixin to.

Well, the old man said. If you-all don't care.

The house the old man entered that morning was no shotgun shack but a mountain cabin of squared logs rent deeply with weather-checks and chinked with clay. It was long and saddle-bowed, divided into two rooms of equal size, and at the far end of one a fireplace of river rock, rocks tumbled smooth as eggs, more ancient than the river itself. From a door to the right a woman's face peered at them furtively as they sat, the taller of the men motioning the old man to a chair cut from a buttertub and padded in hair-worn cowhide. They produced tobacco and papers and passed them to him not ceremoniously but with that deprecatory gesture of humility which country people confer in a look, a lift of the hand. The old man began to feel right homey.

Say you from t'wards Knoxville? the tall man said.

Yessir, he answered, taping down the paper of his cigarette.

I got a sister lives over thataway. Meanest kids I ever seen. Married a boy from Mead's Quarry—you know where that's at?

Shore, the old man said. I come from Red Mountain my ownself. We used to whup Mead's Quarry boys of a Sunday afternoon jest to keep a hand in.

The man grinned. That's what he told me about you-all, he said.

Then the old man grinned.

The other one broke in. Don't reckon you'd keer fer a little drink this early of a mornin?

Not lessen you fellers is fixin to have one.

He disappeared through the door into the lean-to and presently came back with a mason jar. Less see if this here is the one I wanted, he said, tilting it, watching the slow-rising chain of beads. He took off the cap and stretched a draught down his lean corded neck, swallowed deep, cocked his head in a listening attitude, then passed the jar to the old man. That's the one, he said. It's right good drinkin whiskey.

The old man accepted the jar and took a good drink. His legs were beginning to feel a little heavy and he lifted first one and then the other, slightly, testing their weight. He raised the jar again, drank and handed it back to the man. Now that's a right nice little whiskey, he said.

The two men relayed the jar between them and then it was capped and set on the floor. The shorter man was looking out the tiny window. Gettin daylight, he said.

He turned to the old man. You get a right early start, don't ye?

The old man recrossed his legs, taking a look out himself.

Well, he said, kindly early, yes.

You come up from Walland this mornin I reckon?

No, the old man said, Knoxville.

I mean on foot, comin up the mountain . . .

I come straight acrost, the old man said.

They looked at each other. The tall one hesitated a moment, then he said: You say you goin to the Harrykin?

Aim to, the old man said.

Cain't say as it seems like much of a place to jest go to, he said. I've knowed one or two people at different times what was there and would of give some to of been away from it though. Daddy I remember would leave dogs treed there of a night rather'n go in after em. He said they was places you could walk fer half a mile thout ever settin foot to the ground—jest over laurel hells and down timber, and a rattlesnake to the log . . . I never been there myself.

You aimin to stay there long? the other one asked.

But before the old man could answer that, the woman thrust her face through the door and announced breakfast. Both men rose instantly and started for the kitchen, then paused, remembering the old man still seated with the slow words forming on his lips. They had the uneasy look of boys sneaking to table with dirty hands. The old man stood and walked between them, the shorter one smiling a sort of half-smile and saying: I reckon we jest about forgot how to act, ain't we?

Pshaw, said the old man.

At the foot of the mountain the old man found himself in a broad glade grown thick with rushes, a small stream looping placidly over shallow sands stippled with dace shadows, the six-pointed stars of skating waterspiders drifting like bright frail medusas. He squatted and dipped a palmful of water to his lips, watched the dace drift and shimmer. Scout waded past him, elbow-deep into the stream, lapped at it noisily. Strings of red dirt receded from his balding hocks, marbling in the water like blood. The dace skittered into the channel and a watersnake uncurled from a rock at the far bank and glided down the slight current, no more demonstrative of effort or motion than a flute note.

The old man drank and then leaned back against the sledge. The glade hummed softly. A woodhen called from the timber on the mountain and to that sound of all summer days of seclusion and peace the old man slept.

Yessir, the storekeeper said. Yessir, now I believe I do recollect who tis. You some kin of hisn?

No, the man said. No kin. Jest somethin I got to see him about.

He was dressed in clean gray chinos and had a neat felt hat tipped back on his head. Huffaker stole a look out the window to where his car was parked at the side of the porch, a plain black Ford, a late model.

The man saw him look, watched the glint of suspicion narrow the storekeeper's eyes.

Well, Huffaker said, I couldn't tell you offhand where-all you might find him at. He lives up yander somewheres—a random gesture at the brooding hills that cupped in the valley.

He trade here? the man wanted to know.

Well, I couldn't rightly say he did, nosir. Not regular at all. I ain't seen him in here but once or twicet and that's back several week ago. He's a right funny old feller, don't have no money at all I don't reckon.

What'd he buy then?

Well, he got him some backer and a sack of cornmeal. Little sidemeat last time he's in.

He got credit?

Well, no. I don't give out a whole lot of credit. He brings in sang. Ginseng roots. Had some goldenseal too but it ain't worth a whole lot. I give trade on that.

Roots?

Yessir, Huffaker said. I send em off to St. Louis. Same place as I send hides.

The man looked puzzled but he didn't ask any more about that.

You from around here? the storekeeper asked.

From over t'wards Maryville.

Oh, Huffaker said. I got kin over there myself.

He still got that dog?

Who's that?

The old feller . . . the one . . .

Oh. Yessir, did have one with him. A old redbone looked like he'd been drug half to death or warshed in lye one. Didn't have no hair hardly at all. Right pitiful-lookin, like.

Well, the man said, you say you don't know where-all he lives at?

Nosir, I shore don't.

Well, much obliged.

Yessir. You come back.

He did. He came every day for seven days.

He was there next morning early among the un-churched Sunday idlers, hovering on the edge of the circle they formed about the fireless stove, their conviviality so broken by his presence that they took on the look of refugees grimly awaiting bulletins of some current disaster, the news of flood or fire or plague. From time to time he got a drink from the box and stood sipping it, hand on hip, gazing up at the phantasmagoria of merchandise hung about the ceiling beams. Or peered solemnly out the window, beyond the river and the narrow bridge to where a broad green hollow rose and rose into the mountains.

Monday when Huffaker came down he was not there yet but half an hour later when he went out to unlock the gas pump the car was parked on the gravel ramp approaching the store and the man was perched upon the fender in the same creased and tireless clothes sipping coffee from a paper cup. The sun was coming up behind him and to the west fog was breaking, lifting off the slopes to leave the laurel balds burning with the fierce green light of morning. The man was watching again, the peaks across the river, as if with those slategray eyes he might mark out an old man and a hound somewhere on the face of a mountain not less than four miles distant.

When Huffaker let the door to, the man turned. He lifted a palm in greeting and the man nodded. He went down to the pump and undid the lock.

Looks like another purty day, don't it? he called.

Does at that, the man said. He drained the coffee and pitched the cup away, got down from the fender and took a few steps up and down the gravel, stretching himself. Huffaker returned to the store.

Around eleven o'clock he came in, nodding once again to the proprietor. He bought a box of soda crackers and some cheese, looked for a long time at the cake rack and finally took a moonpie. He laid his lunch on the counter and Huffaker began to total it laboriously on a scratch pad, adding the figures aloud.

And a quart of sweet milk, the man said.

He put that down, then went to the cooler and brought back the milk in a quart mason jar. The man looked at it, turned it around on the counter.

That's Mrs Walker's milk, he reassured the man. It's good as ever you drunk, garntee ye.

The man nodded and pulled a clip of bills from his pocket.

Forty-five cents, Huffaker said.

He paid it and went out on the porch where he sat back against a post and ate his lunch. After he had finished he squatted there a long time smoking cigarettes. Then he brought the jar back inside and set it on the counter. Huffaker took it out again and washed it under the tap at the side of the building. Some customers were coming up toward the store and he waved at them and went in.

Later on in the afternoon the man came in again and drank a Coca-Cola. Before he went back out to his car he asked Huffaker what time it was that the old man usually came in.

The old feller?

The one I was astin you about.

Oh. Well, times he come in it was genly of a mornin. But then he don't come regular enough for me to say when a feller be most likely to expect him.

Light gained on the high peaks and in the dawn quiet first birdcalls fell like water on stone. In the wood mists like old gray spirits paled and scattered, by moss coverlets the dark earth stirred and nightfurled wildflowers unbent their withered fronds all down the path where came the derelict hound shambling along in an aureole of its own incredibility, the old man picking his steps over the schist and quartz chines, his hex-cane bobbing lightly on his shoulder, carrying a limp and greasy paper bag of the curious twisted roots with which he bartered. They crossed a broad rock slide emblazoned with sun and threaded by a trickle of water in a rock channel rusted copper-dark. The old man paused to scale a slate down into the gorge where trees lay tossed and broken. The dog peered down, looked at the old man inquisitively, studied the empty gorge again and then moved on, the old man taking up his cane and following. The sole of his brogan was all but off now and he limped, favoring the odd shoe to save the binder twine with which he had tied it together.

Crossing the slide they entered the deep woods once more, the sun winnowed in tall fans among the spiring trunks, greengold and black vermiculated on the forest floor. With his cane the old man felled regiments of Indian Pipe, poked the green puffballs to see the smoke erupt in a poisonous verdant cloud. The woods were damp with the early morning and now and again he could hear the swish of a limb where a squirrel jumped and the beaded patter of water-drops in the leaves. Twice they flushed mountain pheasants, Scout sidestepping nervously as they roared up out of the laurel.

The path the old man took was a fire trail that had been built by the C C C. From the glade in which he now made his home he had to climb nearly a thousand feet to reach it, but once on the trail the walking was easy and excepting the injured shoe he would have swung along at a good pace. It was six miles to the river where he crossed and came to the highway and the same ubiquitous crossroads store with the drunken porch, the huge and rock-battered Nehi signs, the weather-curled laths, the paintless stonecolored wood—but the old man had taken an early start. Through a gap in the trees he could see the valley far below him where the river ran, a cauldron in the mountain's shadow where smoke and spume seethed like the old disturbance of the earth erupting once again, black mist languid in the cuts and trenches as flowing lava and the palisades of rock rising in the high-shored rim beyond the valley—and beyond the valley, circling the distant hoary cupolas now standing into morning, the sun, reaching to the slope where the old man rested, speared mist motes emblematic as snowflakes and broke them down in spangled and regimental disorder, reached the trees and banded them in light, struck weftwork in the slow un-curling ferns—the sun in its long lightfall recoiled again in leafwater.

Brogan and cane and cracked pad clatter and slide on the shelly rocks and stop where a snake lies curled belly-up to the silent fold and dip of a petal-burst of butterflies fanning his flat and deadwhite underside. Scout smells cautiously at the snake, the butterflies in slow riot over his head, flowery benediction of their veined and harlequin wings. With his cane the old man turns the snake, remarking the dusty carpet pattern of its dull skin, the black clot of blood where the rattles have been cut away.

They go on—steps soft now in the rank humus earth, or where carapaced with lichens the texture of old green velvet, or wet and spongy earth tenoned with roots, the lecherous ganglia of things growing—coming down, pursuing the shadowline into the smoking river valley.

Huffaker would have said it was by chance that he happened to be looking out the window toward the river the morning the old man came, but he had been watching not much less keenly than the patient and taciturn visitor in the pressed gray chinos. So he had been looking for him for a week and there he was on

the bridge with the crudely carved staff, carrying a
small paper bag in his hand, a moldy crokersack tied
at his waist in front like an immense and disreputable
sporran, and the wreckage of dog padding at his heels,
raising its bitten muzzle into the air from time to time
in a sort of hopeless and indomitable affirmation—pro-
ceeding on the weathered sun-washed bridge, jaunty and
yet sad, like maimed soldiers returning. Huffaker stepped
to the door and the man, coming from the car with
slow bootcrunch in the gravel, shot him a quick look.
Huffaker walked to the broken thermometer on the
tin snuff sign at the corner of the store and pretended
to check it, gazed at the mounting sun and sniffed at the
air, went back in. The old man was on the road,
coming toward the store. The man was standing on
the porch with one arm hooked loosely about a post,
his forefinger in his watchpocket, chewing a straw
slowly and watching his approach with the composed
disinterest of a professional assassin.

The old man climbed onto the porch and the man
said:

Arthur Ownby.

Arthur Ownby's eyes swam slowly across, fixed upon
him.

Yessir, he said.

Get in that car over yonder. Let's go.

The old man had stopped. He was looking at the
man, and then he was looking past him, eyes milk-blue
and serene, studying the dipping passage of a dove, and
beyond, across the canted fields of grass to the green
mountain, and to the thin blue peaks rising into the
distant sky with no crestline of shape or color to stop
them, ascending forever.

You hear?

The old man turned. You don't keer if I trade first, do ye? he said.

You're under arrest. You don't need to trade nothin.

The old man turned back toward the store with an empty gesture, holding the sack of ginseng in his hand.

Let's go, the man said again.

So he started down off the porch with a forlorn air and the dog, bland, patient, turning behind him with myopic and near-senseless habituation until, led by the man in the starched and rattling clothes, they reached the car. The man swung the door open and the old man fumbled and climbed his way onto the front seat. As the door was closing it began to occur to him that the dog was still out and apparently not under arrest as he was and he flailed violently at the glass and upholstery swinging toward him and checked it. The man looked at him questioningly.

He didn't know how to begin so he sat there for part of a minute with his jaw going up and down as if he couldn't breathe and the man said, Well, what now?

The old man nodded his head to where in the gravel the ancient hound stood gazing up at the machine before him with a baffled look. What about him? the old man said.

What about him?

Well, you don't keer if he rides, do ye?

You're resistin arrest, Ownby, now get on in there. He slammed the door but the old man's cane was hanging over the runningboard and in mutual defeat the door rocked open again as the cane cracked. The old man pulled it in the car with him and studied the lower part of it, stooping to examine the whiskers of wood standing up from the break. The man slapped the door again and it bounded in snugly upon the old man and all but took his breath.

The man was coming around the car and he hadn't much more time so he pulled at the handles and got the right one and opened the door again and leaned out and called to the dog, standing off a few feet now and rocking back and forth in consternation.

Hya, Scout, the old man whispered. Come on, get in here.

Hey! the man called. What in the hell you think you're up to now?

The dog started, backed away. The man paused midway in his passage from door to door, returned. The old man straightened up and watched him come.

I told you oncet, the man said, coming up fast and reaching for the door. The old man recoiled, waiting for it to buffet shut against him, but instead it wrenched outward and the man's face jutted in and stared at him in a mask of classic anger. You tryin to excape? he wanted to know.

Nosir, the old man said. I was jest gettin my dog in . . .

Jest what! Dog? He turned and seemed to see the hound for the first time. They said you's crazy. Dog's ass, you cain't take no dog . . .

He cain't shift for hisself, the old man said. He's too old.

I ain't no dog catcher and this ain't no kennel, the man said. And I wadn't sent here to haul no broken-down sooner around. Now get in the goddamned car and stay put. He said it very slowly and evenly and the old man really began to worry. But he suffered the door closed to once more and didn't mention it again until the man came around and got in beside him.

It wouldn't hurt nothin for him to ride, he said. I cain't hardly leave him jest a-standin there.

Old-timer, the man said, I advise you jest to set still

and hush up cause you in plenty of trouble already. He cranked the engine and slid the gearshift upward and the old man felt himself rocketed backward violently with a welter of dust boiling and receding before him and the dog standing there in the drive with the gravel dancing about him and then they cut one long rattling curve and were on the road and leaving, and the old man, clutching his cane, holding the dirty little sack between his knees, looked back at the dog still standing there like some atavistic symbol or brute herald of all questions ever pressed upon humanity and beyond understanding, until the dog raised his head to clear the folds above his milky eyes and set out behind them at a staggering trot.

Warn blew little cone-shaped thistles into the fur. No, he said. Ten maybe. See here —he blew again, cotton mink. Takes a first-class mink to bring twenty dollars.

The boy nodded.

Fur's slippin, Warn said. Whew, here. He handed the mink back. Sure raised hell with it, didn't he?

The boy took it and pitched it underhand back up onto the shelf in the woodshed. He clambered down the pile of logs and they went out together. Some wasps were hovering beneath the eaves with their long legs dangling. Small buds already on the locust trees. It would soon be nothing but bones, but he wouldn't come to see, like when he dug up the flying squirrel he had buried in a jar and found only bones with bits of fur rolling around inside the glass like bed-lint.

They took the road to Warn's house, the fields still
too wet to cross, passed the store.

You got any money? Warn asked him.

No, he said. I ain't sold my hides yet. You?

Naw. I sold my hides but I ain't got nothin left. I
blow it in quick as I get it. Got me some new shoes for
school is about all.

What you get for em?

For the hides? I don't know; two dollars on most of
em. That big rat got three I think it was and some of
em the man said was kits and they didn't bring but a
dollar. I had eighteen hides and I think it come to thirty-
one dollars.

I should get six dollars, the boy said. I owe out two.

Who you owe?

Sylder. He loant me the money for traps when Gifford got mine. I'd done signed a paper to buy em
uptown—on account of the man let me have those first
ones I bought at lot price.

You keep messin with Sylder and signing papers uptown and sech shit as that and you goin to get your ass
slung in the jail after all. Lucky Gifford didn't do it.

Gifford's chickenshit.

Oh, Warn said. I didn't know you had him scared
of you.

Warn had his own room in the back of the house.
The boy sat on the bed while he went through the top
drawer of an old-fashioned sewing cabinet. He dredged
up: a hawkbill knife, three arrowheads, a collection of
rifle-balls velvety gray with oxidation, a scalpel, rocks,
some dynamite caps, miscellaneous pieces of fishing
tackle, dried ginseng, a roll of copper wire . . . Rifling
through the mass he at length came up with a thin and
dog-eared pamphlet, its cover decorated with an archaic
and ill-proportioned ink sketch of a trapped lynx. Across

the top in black script was the title TRAPPING THE FUR BEARERS OF NORTH AMERICA. Warn handled the treasure reverently. I got this from Uncle Ather, he said. It'll have something in it.

Under a section entitled *Lynx and Bobcat Sets* they found a plan of such devious cunning as appealed to their minds. The bait was to be suspended from a limb and overhanging a stump. The trap would be set on top of the stump, so that when the victim stood—the illustration depicted a great hairy lynx sniffing at the bait on hind legs—his paw would come to rest on the stump and so into the trap—also illustrated, in broken-line, straining beneath a handful of leaves.

Warn nodded in solemn approval. That's the one, he said. The boy studied the set carefully and then Warn tucked the book away in the sewing cabinet.

You reckon it really was a bobcat?

I don't know what-all else it could of been, Warn said. Ain't nothin else around here got sharp claws that I know of.

I sure could of used that ten dollars, the boy said.

The desk sergeant studied Marion Sylder's angular frame with a hurt look, as if he were being put upon. Sylder looked back at him with a suggestion of good humor. The desk sergeant rebent his head to his papers, his lips working in patient disgust. He pondered for some minutes, replaced a folder in the filing drawer of the desk and reached for a pen. Name, he said, gazing at the inkstand with weary boredom.

Fred Long.

Marion Paris Sylder. Occupation.

Iron and steel . . .

None. Married?

No.

Married. Address.

Red Mountain Tennessee.

Route Nine, Knoxville. Mm . . . Age.

Twenty.

—eight. Previous convictions.

Silence.

Previous convictions.

The sergeant looked up at Sylder as if surprised to see him there. Previous convictions, he said again, slowly.

Again a moment or two of silence. Far to the rear of the building a remote clanking sound. The sergeant waited. Then he nodded wearily to the patrolman sitting in a chair by the door. The man rose and sauntered over to the prisoner, something of the laconical about him. Sylder turned to look at him. When he turned back to the man at the desk the patrolman jabbed his night-stick into his ribs.

Ow! Sylder said.

The patrolman looked aggrieved.

Previous convictions, droned the sergeant, stifling a yawn.

You seem to know all about it, Sylder said. Oof!

The patrolman studied his face with an eager look, holding the stick in readiness again.

Previous con—

None, Sylder said.

None.

The sergeant leaned back with closed eyes, a rapt and serene look. The patrolman returned to his post at the door. From the cells to the rear of the building came bits and pieces of a sad voice singing. The sergeant turned papers over. In the outer corridor men were coming in, stamping their feet and rattling their raincoats, cussing the weather. A furnace pipe clattered.

At length the sergeant regarded Sylder again. I reckon that's all for now, he said. You're booked on illegal possession—untaxed. I got somebody comin down wants to see you, have a little talk kindly.

Who's that? Sylder said.

Fella name of Gifford. Ever hear of him?

Jailer!

Sylder's third visitor was the boy, wide-eyed and serious before the smirking usherance of the jailer.

Here's your uncle, the jailer said. Little buddy come a-callin.

The boy stared at the man seated on the steel bunk. The jailer followed his gaze. Well now, he said, he don't seem too peart, does he? Looks kindly like he's been sortin cats. Step on in and say howdy. Cheer the poor feller up some.

The boy stepped in. Sylder's eyes focused onto him, he managed a small grin, a nod. Howdy there, Hogjowls, he said. The door rattled to behind them, the jailer departing, heelclack, keyjangle, echoing down the corridor.

Howdy, said the boy. What happent to you?

Well, I had a little disagreement with these fellers . . . as to whether a man can haul untaxed whiskey over tax-kept roads or whether by not payin the whiskey tax he forfeits the privilege of drivin over the roads the whiskey don't keep up that ain't taxed or if it was would be illegal anyway. I think what they do is deeport you.

No, the boy said, I mean . . . you wreck?

Oh. No . . . I was wrecked all right, but I didn't wreck. He fingered sorely the particolored swellings on his cheek and forehead. Kindly a bang-up job, ain't it?

Mutual acquaintance helped out with the decoratin . . .
the deacon Gifford. With two buddies to hold me.
Wadn't even much spirited about it till I kicked him in
the nuts. Now they got to worry about gettin me
unswole so as I can appear in court. I got some busted
ribs too that they don't know about yet. I'm sort of
holdin em for a ace. Here, set down. He grimaced and
dropped his feet down off the bed to clear a seat.

The boy hadn't said anything else. He lowered himself onto the bunk, still staring at Sylder. Then he said:

That son of a bitch.

Ah, said Sylder.

How'd they . . . you said you never wrecked, how
did they . . .

Catch me? It wadn't hard. I had my choice though, I
could of jumped off the bridge. They live ever oncet
in a while.

What?

Water in the gas. A little too much rain, I reckon.
Too much for old Eller's leaky-assed tank leastways.
There's one bill the son of a bitch'll play hell collectin.
—It quit in the middle of the Henley Street Bridge.

Oh.

Sylder had leaned back against the concrete wall and
was tapping a cigarette from its package. Ain't that a hell
of a note? he said.

I'll get him.

Hmm?

I'm goin to get the son of a bitch.

What! That old fart? Why I'll be dipped in . . .
Then he said Oh.

That's right, the boy said. The deacon.

The smile had fallen from Sylder's face. Wait a
minute, he said. You don't get nobody.

Him, the boy said.

No, Sylder said. He was looking very hard at the boy but the boy knew he was in the right.

Why? he said.

You jest stay away from Jefferson Gifford, that's all. You hear?

You jest think I'll get in trouble, the boy said. That I . . .

Stubborn little bastard, ain't you? Look.

Sylder paused, he seemed to be trying to think of something, a word perhaps. Look, he said, what's between him and me is between him and me. It don't need nobody else. So I thank ye kindly but no thank ye, you don't owe me nothin and I ain't crippled. I'll tend to my own Giffords. All right?

The boy didn't answer, didn't seem to be listening. Sylder lit the cigarette and watched him. He turned and looked once at Sylder and then he seemed to remember something and he reached into the watchpocket of his jeans and took out two folded dollar bills and handed them to him.

What's that? Sylder said.

The two dollars I owe you. That you loant me for traps.

Naw . . . Sylder started. Then he stopped and looked at the boy still holding out the two dirty bills. Okay, he said. He took the money and crammed it into his shirtpocket. Okay, that makes us square.

The boy was silent for a minute. Then he said:

No.

No what?

No it don't make us square. Because maybe I lost the traps on your account but that's okay and I earned em back and paid for em and that's okay . . . but you got beat up on my account and maybe in jail too that . . .

and that's why it ain't square yet, that part of it not
square.

Sylder started to reach for the money, thought better
of it and sat up, grinding the cigarette out beneath his
heel. Then he looked at the boy. Square be damned, he
said. I ast you to stay away from Gifford, that's all.
Will you?

The boy didn't say anything.

Swear it? Sylder said.

No.

Sylder watched him, the still childish face set with
truculent purpose. Look, he said, you're fixin to get
me in worse trouble than I already am, you . . .

I won't get no . . .

No, wait a damn minute.

He did. They sat looking at each other, the man's face
misshapen as if bee-stung, him leaning forward gaunt
and huge and the boy perched delicately on the edge
of the metal pallet as if loath to sit too easily where so
many had lain in such hard rest.

Look, Sylder said, taking a long breath, you want to
talk about square, all right. Me and Gif are square.

The boy looked at him curiously.

Yes, he said. I busted him and he busted me. That's
fair, ain't it?

The boy was still silent, calmly incredulous.

No, Sylder went on, I ain't forgettin about jail. You
think because he arrested me that thows it off again
I reckon? I don't. It's his job. It's what he gets paid
for. To arrest people that break the law. And I didn't
jest break the law, I made a livin at it. He leaned forward and looked the boy in the face. More money in
three hours than a workin man makes in a week. Why is
that? Because it's harder work? No, because a man who
makes a livin doin somethin that has to get him in jail

sooner or later has to be paid for the jail, has to be paid in advance not jest for his time breakin the law but for the time he has to build when he gets caught at it. So I been paid. Gifford's been paid. Nobody owes nobody. If it wadn't for Gifford, the law, I wouldn't of had the job I had blockadin and if it wadn't for me blockadin, Gifford wouldn't of had his job arrestin blockaders. Now who owes who?

His voice was beginning to rise and he had about him a look almost furious. But you, he went on, you want to be some kind of a goddamned hero. Well, I'll tell ye, they ain't no more heroes.

The boy seemed to shrink, his face flushing.

You understand that? Sylder said.

I never claimed I wanted to be no hero, the boy said sullenly.

Nobody never claimed it, Sylder said. Anyway I never done nothin on your account like you said. I don't do nothin I don't want to. You want to do me a favor jest stay away from Gifford. Stay away from me too. You ought not to of come here. You'll get me charged with delinquency to a minor. Go on now.

He leaned back against the wall and stared at the emptiness before him. After a while the boy got up and went to the door and tried it, and Sylder, not looking up or speaking to the boy, called for the jailer. He heard him come and the clank of keys, the cell door grating open. Then quiet. He looked up. The boy was standing in the doorway, half turned, looking at him with a wan smile, puzzled, like one who aspires to disbelief in the face of immutable fact. Sylder lifted one hand in farewell. Then the door clanged to.

He sat up, half rose from the cot, would call him back to say *That's not true what I said. It was a damned lie ever word. He's a rogue and a outlaw hisself and you're welcome to shoot him, burn him down in his bed, any damn thing, because he's a traitor to boot and maybe a man steals from greed or murders in anger but he sells his own neighbors out for money and it's few lie that deep in the pit, that far beyond the pale.*

Softly and with slow grace her leathered footpads fell, hind tracking fore with a precision profoundly feline, a silken movement where her shoulders rolled, haunches swayed. Belly swaying slightly too, lean but pendulous. Head low and divorced of all but linear motion, as if fixed along an unseen rail. A faint musty odor still clung to her, odor of the outhouse where she had slept all day, restless in the heat and languishing among the dusty leaves in the corner, listening to the dry scratch and slither of roaches, the interstitial boring of wood-beetles. Now she came down the patch obscure with parched weeds shedding thin blooms of sifting dust where she brushed them. At dusk-dark from her degenerate habitation, emerging to make her way down the narrow patch as cats go.

She passed through the honeysuckles by a dark tunnel where the earth still held moisture, down the bank to a culvert by which she crossed beneath the road and came into a field and into a dry gully, the cracked and curling clay like a paving of potsherds, and turned up an artery of the wash, grown here with milkweed and burdock. following a faint aura of vole or shrew, until she came to a small burrow in the grasses. She scratched at the matted whorl, caved it in and trod it down, moved on across the field, crickets scuttling, grasshoppers springing from their weed-stems and whirring away. A shadow passed soundlessly overhead, perhaps a flock of late-returning birds.

Near the center of the field was a single walnut tree bedded in a crop of limestone which had so far fended it against axe and plowshare. Among these rocks she nosed, in their small labyrinths undulant as a ferret. Odor of walnuts and ground squirrels. But she found nothing.

When she left the rocks, was clear of the overreaching branches of the tree, there grew about her a shadow in the darkness like pooled ink spreading, a soft-hissing feathered sound which ceased even as she half turned, saw unbelieving the immense span of wings cupped downward, turned again, already squalling when the owl struck her back like a falling rock.

Mr Eller closed the lionheaded door behind him and rattled the latch to see that it was secure. Then he checked the plaited fob on the notecase in his hip pocket, adjusted his straw hat, and started up the road toward the house. At the mailbox he was arrested by the high thin wail of a cat coming apparently from straight overhead. He looked up but there were no trees there. He shook his head and went on, stepping carefully in the gutted drive. The squall sounded once more, this time more distant and to the ridge of pines behind the house. He continued on, to the porch where a yellow bulb held forth its dull steadfast light, to a place of surcease.

A young social worker recently retained by the Knox County Welfare Bureau, having been notified through his office of the detention of one aged and impecunious gentleman at the county jail pending hearing of his case (charges ranging from Destruction of Government Property to Assault with Intent to Kill) proceeded to make such investigation as would determine whether the gentleman had relatives, and if not, to what department or agency he might properly be assigned as ward. The agent, having been admitted into the cell where the elderly gentleman was confined, addressed him:

Mr Ownby?

Yessir.

I represent the Welfare Bureau for the county.

Welfare?

Yes. We . . . you see, we help people.

The old man turned that over in his mind. He didn't seem to be paying much attention to the thin young man standing just inside the door. He scratched his jaw and then he said, Well, I ain't got nothin. I don't reckon I can hep yins any.

The agent made a fleeting effort at comprehension, passed it over. All we need, he said, is some information.

The old man turned and looked at him. You another policeman? he asked.

No, said the agent. I represent the Welfare Bureau for . . . I have been asked to see you—to see if perhaps we can help you in any way.

Well, the old man said, I kindly doubt it. I'm what you might call Brushy bound.

Yes, said the agent. I mean . . . you see, Mr Ownby, there are certain benefits to which you may be entitled. You seem to have been overlooked by our department for some time and we would like to have a record of your case for our, our, records, you see. And so I have some forms here that I need your help in filling out.

Hmm, the old man said.

Do you mind answering a few questions?

Don't reckon, the old man said. Here, set down.

Thank you, said the agent. He lowered himself gingerly onto the cot and began to unstrap his briefcase. His hand disappeared inside and emerged with a sheaf of printed forms intershuffled with carbon paper. Now, he said comfortably, first of all, your age.

Well, I don't rightly know.

Yes. I beg your pardon?

Don't know for sure, that is. There's a part of it I don't remember too good.

Well, could you tell us when you were born?

The old man eyed him curiously. If I knowed that,

he said patiently, I could figure how old I was. And tell us that.

The agent smiled weakly. Yes. Of course. Well, could you estimate your age then? You are over sixty-five?

Considerable.

Well, about how old would you say?

It ain't about, the old man said, it's either. Either eighty-three or eighty-four.

The agent wrote that down on his form, studied it for a moment with satisfaction. Fine, he said. Now, where is your present residence?

If'n I'm eighty-four I'll live to be a hunerd and five providin I get to eighty-five.

Yes. Your . . .

When was you born?

The agent looked up from his forms. Nineteen-thirteen, he said, but we . . .

What date?

June. The thirteenth. Mr Ownby . . .

The old man tilted his eyes upward in reflection. Hmm, he said. That was a Friday. Kindly a bad start. Was your daddy over twenty-eight when you was born?

No, please, Mr Ownby. These questions, you see . . .

The old man hushed and the agent sat watching him for a minute. Now, he said. Your present address?

Well, the old man said, I did live on Forked Creek —Twin Fork Road, but I moved to the mountains. I got me a little place up there.

Where is that?

That's all right where it's at.

But we have to have an address, Mr Ownby.

Well, put down Twin Fork Road then, the old man said.

You live alone?

Jest me and Scout. Or we did.

Scout?

Dog.

The agent continued to write. You have, I believe, no family or relatives.

Yessir.

The agent looked up. Well, he said, we'll need their names then.

I mean yes I don't have none, the old man said wearily.

The agent continued with his questions, the old man answering yes or no or giving information. Upturned upon his knee his right hand opened and closed with a kneading action, as though he were trying to soften something in his palm. Until at length it stopped and the old man sat upright, fist clenched and quivering and the veins like old blue thread imprinted in the paper skin, sat erect and cut the agent off with a question of his own:

Why don't you say what you come here to say? Why not jest up and ast me?

I beg your pardon? said the agent.

Why I done it. Rung shells and shot your hootnanny all to hell? Where *you* from, heh? You talk like a God-damned yankee. What you do for a livin? Ast questions?

Mr Ownby . . .

Mr Ownby's ass. I could tell you why—and you stit wouldn't know. That's all right. You can set and ast a bunch of idjit questions. But not knowin a thing ain't never made it not so. Well, I'm a old man and I've seen some hard times, so I don't reckon Brushy Mountain'll be the worst place I was ever in.

Mr Ownby, I'm sure you're upset and I assure you . . .

Ahh, said the old man.

Mr Ownby, there are only a few more questions. If you'd like I could come back another time. I . . . We at the agency feel . . .

I reckon you could, the old man said. I ain't goin
nowhere. He leaned back against the wall and passed
one hand across his eyes as if to wipe away some image.
Then he sat very still with his hands on his knees, his
shaggy head against the bricks, restored to patience and
a look of tried and inviolate sanctity, the faded blue eyes
looking out down the row of cages, a forest of sweating
iron dowels, forms of men standing or huddled upon
their pallets, and the old man felt the circle of years
closing, the final increment of the curve returning him
again to the inchoate, the prismatic flux of sound and
color wherein he had drifted once before and now beyond the world of men. By the time the agent had
gathered his forms and tucked them once again into his
briefcase the old man had closed his eyes and the agent
called quietly for the jailer and left him.

The jailer walked with him down the corridor. The
agent had regained his composure. Well, he said cheerily,
he's a cantankerous old rascal, isn't he?

The old feller? I reckon. Been pretty quiet here, but
then they shore had a time gettin him here.

How's that? said the agent.

Why, he shot four men. Luther Boyd's stit hoppin
around on crutches.

Did he kill anyone? the agent asked.

No, but it wadn't from not tryin. That old man's
ornery enough.

Yes, the agent said, musing. Definitely an anomic
type.

Mean as a snake, said the jailer. Here, watch the door.

The agent thanked the desk sergeant as he passed
through the outer room. He swung the briefcase to his
left hand and dabbled his handkerchief upon his forehead. Over the worn runner on the flagged hall floor his
steps were soundless and he moved with a slender grace
of carriage, delicate and feline.

In the spring of the year you may see them about the grounds walking or sitting perhaps in the wake and swath of the droning mowers lifting up strewn daisyheads white and torn, softly fallen in the grass. Long monologues rise and fall, they speak of great deeds and men and noble eras gone. The mowers return along the fence in martial formation drowning the babble of voices.

The brick buildings atop the hill are dark with age, formidable yet sad, like old fortress ruins. Families come from the reception room into the pale sun, moving slowly, talking, grieving their silent griefs. The unvisited amble hurriedly about the grounds like questing setters, gesticulant and aimless.

There are others who sit quietly and unattended in the grass watching serene and childlike with serious eyes. Tender voices caress their ears endlessly and they

are beyond sorrow. Some wave hopefully to the passing
cars of picnickers and bathers. The eldest of all sits a
little apart, a grass stem revolving between his yellowed
teeth, remembering in the summer.

The mountain road brick-red of dust laced with lizard
tracks, coming up through the peach orchard, hot, wind-
less, cloistral in a silence of no birds save one vulture
hung in the smokeblue void of the sunless mountainside,
rocking on the high updrafts, and the road turning and
gated with bullbriers waxed and green, and the green ca-
daver grin sealed in the murky waters of the peach pit,
slimegreen skull with newts coiled in the eyesockets and
a wig of moss.

The old man paused at the door, the attendant leading him by one arm through and into the room apparently against his will, peered at the boy through
slotted lids as if unused to light of any intensity. He
looked older than the boy remembered him. The attendant pulled him into the room, him shuffling in the
old brogans with the paper-thin soles, a rasping sound
on the concrete floor.

They came over to where the boy sat. Here's your
nephew, the attendant said loudly into the old man's
ear. You remember him?

The old man flashed a glint of blue eyes from deep
beneath the closing lids. I reckon, he said.

The attendant pushed him down into the wicker chair
next to the boy and left them, going back through the
door, high squeak of crepe diminishing in the corridor.
The old man sat in his chair staring across at the un-
relieved spanse of whitewashed plaster.

Uncle Ather?

He turned. The boy was holding at him a huge bag
of chewing tobacco.

I brought you some tobacca, he said. Beech-Nut, like you like.

The old man took it from him slowly and slid it inside his shirtfront. Thank ye, son, he said. I'm much obliged.

They sat quietly. The mowers passed again beneath the window, droning louder and then fading. Laughter and distant voices, someone crying, quite softly, like a child who is just lonely.

Kindly warmin up a little, ain't it? the old man said.

We had a little rain out to the mountain, the boy said. Sunday week I believe it was.

Yes, the old man said. Well, be little of it this year I reckon. Done had it all at oncet. They's a good warm spell comin on. Won't nothin make, won't nothin keep. A seventh year is what it is.

He gazed at the floor between his shoes, out of the bell-flared tops his shinbones rising hairless, pale and polished as shafts of driftwood and into his trouser legs. Get older, he said, you don't need to count. You can read the signs. You can feel it in your ownself. Knowed a blind man oncet could tell lots of things afore they happent. But it'll be hot and dry. Late frost is one sign if you don't know nothin else. So they won't but very little make because folks thinks that stuff grows by seasons and it don't. It goes by weather. Game too, and folks themselves if they knowed it. I recollect one winter, I was jest a young feller, they wadn't no winter. Not hardly a frost even. It was a sight in the world the things that growed. That was a seventh year seventh and you'll be old as me afore it comes again.

The old man paused, consulted a trouser button. Then he said: I look for this to be a bad one. I look for real calamity afore this year is out.

When the boy asked him the old man explained that

there was a lean year and a year of plenty every seven years. The boy thought about it. Then he said: That makes it ever fourteen year then, don't it?

Well, said the old man, depends on how you count I reckon. If'n you count jest the lean and not the plenty, or the other way around, I reckon you could call it ever fourteen year. I reckon some folks might figure that-away. I call it the seventh my ownself.

He gazed at the wall above the line of wicker chairs. The attendant passed through the room with a young man and a woman. She was drying her eyes with a yellow lace handkerchief. They went out. After a while the boy said:

They got Marion Sylder.

The old man turned his head, the fine white silk of his hair lifting slightly with the motion as if a breeze had touched it. Who's that? he said.

Sylder. The . . . the feller used to haul whiskey for Hobie. They caught him with a load and sent him to Brushy.

Thought his name was Jack, the old man said.

No, Sylder. Marion Sylder. He was a friend of mine.

Yes, the old man said. I recollect seein him on the mountain time or two. Had a black car. Kindly a new one I believe it was. Say they sent him to Brushy.

Three years. For runnin whiskey.

That's pitiful, the old man said. Feller nowadays you don't get by with much. Yes, I recollect the boy, don't know as I ever did meet him. Well, I hope he fares better'n me. I cain't get used to all these here people. The old man looked like he might be going to say more but he stopped and he looked at the boy, his wiry and tufted brows bunched whether in pain or anger and eyes blanched with age a china-blue, but fierce, a visage hoary and peregrine.

How long do you have to . . . stay in?

Here? he said, looking about him. Likely a good while, son. They ain't never said what I was charged with nor nothin but I suspicion they think me light in the head is what it is. I reckon you knowed this was a place for crazy people. What they tend to do with me when they come to find out I ain't crazy I couldn't speculate. He patted the front of his shirt where he had put the tobacco. How's young Pulliam? he said.

He's gone up in the country to stay with his grammaw, the boy said. Ain't nobody much left around no more.

No, the old man said. He ever catch him a mink?

No. I caught one though.

Did, eh? What did it bring?

It never brought nothin. They was a bobcat or somethin got aholt of it and tore it up.

That's a shame, said the old man. Did ye lay ye a set for that old cat?

Me and Warn did. But we never caught nothin but a big old possum.

Cats is smart, allowed the old man. Course it could of been a common everday housecat. They'll tear up anything they come up on, a cat will. Housecats is smart too. Smarter'n a dog or a mule. Folks thinks they ain't on account of you cain't learn em nothin, but what it is is that they won't learn nothin. They too smart. Knowed a man oncet had a cat could talk. Him and this cat'd talk back and forth of one another like ary two people. That's one cat I kept shy of. I knowed what it was. Lots of times that happens, a body dies and their soul takes up in a cat for a spell. Specially somebody drownded or like that where they don't get buried proper.

But not for no longer than seven year so he would be

gone now and I don't have to fool with him no more
except he ought not to of got burnt, that ought not to
of happent and maybe I done wrong in that way to of
let that happen, but it's done now and he's gone, that
had to of been him Eller was supposed to of heard, won-
derin what all it could of been squallin thataway, not
that I'd of told anybody—him leavin out cat and all and
bound most probably for hell and I hope they don't
nobody hear no more from him never. So that man put
him there either justified or not is free too afore God
because after that seven year they cain't nobody bother
you, what that lawyer said and I had been scoutin nine
year he said was two year longer than needful but this
time I was too old and they catched me.

Yes, he said, they's lots of things folks don't know
about sech as that. Cats is a mystery, always has been.
He stopped, passed a hand across his face dreamily.
Then he turned to the boy. Believe you've growed some,
ain't ye? he said.

The boy ran his palms along his knees. I reckon, he
said.

Mm hm, the old man said. What do you figure you'll
make?

I don't know, he said. Not much of nothin.

Well, the old man said, it's always hard for a young
feller to get a start. Does seem like they's any number
of ways to get money nowadays, not like when I was
growin up cash money was right hard to come by.
They's even a bounty on findin dead bodies, man over
to Knoxville does pretty good grapplehookin em when
they jump off of the bridge like they do there all the
time. They tell me he gets out fast enough to beat anybody else to em only not so fast as they might stit be
a-breathin. So they tell it leastways.

But I never done it to benefit myself because I knowed

*I'd have to scout the bushes if they found I done it as I
allowed they would and if I did have my reasons stit
they cain't a man say I done it to benefit myself.*

A man gets older, he said, he finds they's lots of things
he can do jest as well without and so he don't have to
worry about this and that the way a young feller will.
I worked near all my life and never had nothin. Seems
like a old man'd be allowed his rest but then he comes
to find they's things you have to do on account of nobody else wants to attend to em. Like that would make
em go away. And maybe they don't look like much but
then they lead you around like you might start a rabbit
dog to hunt a fence-corner and get drug over half the
county against nightfall. Which a old man ain't good
at noway. He eased himself slightly in the chair and
shifted his weight. Most ever man loves peace, he said,
and none better than a old man.

*Or even knows they need attendin to. But I never
done it to benefit myself. Shot that thing. Like I kept
peace for seven year sake of a man I never knowed nor
seen his face and like I seen them fellers never had no
business there and if I couldn't run em off I could anyway let em know they was one man would let on that
he knowed what they was up to. But I knowed if they
could build it they could build it back and I done it
anyway. Ever man loves peace and a old man best of all.*

Do they allow you to chew in here?

I kindly doubt it, the old man said. I ain't a-fixin to
ast noway. I'll jest slip me one when I see clear to.
They's some in here I wouldn't put past tellin on a
feller. Half loonies. The real loonies wouldn't. Some
here that ain't crazy, like me, but I doubt they'd want
to tell.

I wonder how come them to be here, the boy said.

The old man ran a lank and corded hand through his

hair. I couldn't say, he said. The ways of these people is strange to me. I did mean to ast you, you ain't seen my old dog I don't reckon?

No, the boy said, I've not seen him. You want I could go out to your place and hunt him.

Well, ever you're out thataway might holler for him. I don't know what to tell ye to do with him. I ain't got no money to ast nobody to feed him with and I couldn't shoot him was he too poor to walk, but might could somebody else . . .

I see him I'll take care of him, the boy said. I wouldn't charge you nothin noway.

Well, the old man said, refolding his hands in his lap. They looked up together, an orderly crossing the room with prim steps and bearing in tow an odor of disinfectant, cleaning fluid redolent of sassafras from the corridor where two Negroes mopped backwards toward each other. They could hear the measured slap of the mops on the baseboard above the door's long pneumatic hiss until it closed and they sat again in quiet, the sunlight strong and airy in the room.

That wasn't the one. He said:

What are these? the stethoscope still about his neck and jerking about rubbery when he moved.

Shotgun done it, said the old man, seated half naked and in decorous rectitude upon the examining table with his feet just clearing the floor and looking straight ahead —so that the intern had moved him about roughly without speaking either as you might a cataleptic wasted thin with years until the old man had asked him quietly if he intended to kill him.

What were you doing, robbing a henhouse?

The old man didn't answer. He said again:

I know she's here.

If she is she don't want to see you.

I mean to see her.

Then the barrel of the gun shortening and withdraw-ing in the cup of his shoulder and his face bent to the stock and him walking into it, the black plume of smoke forming soundlessly about the muzzle and the shot pop-ping into his leg, audible and painless in his flesh and him taking another step with the same leg and pitching forward as if he had stepped in a hole and then he could hear the shot.

You reckon you'll come back to the mountain, the boy said. When you . . . come back?

Oh, said the old man, well. Yes. Yes, most likely I will. I allowed I might go back up yander in the mountains where my new place is at but I don't know as I will. A man gets lonesome off by hisself he ain't used to it. I spect I'll jest come on back if the old house ain't fell down. Yes.

He shuffled his feet on the floor. A shadow fell over them and he looked up to see the boy standing. Are ye leavin? he said.

Yes, the boy said. I got to get on back.

Well. I thank ye for the tobacca.

It's all right.

Well.

I'll come again.

No, the old man said.

Yes. I will.

Well.

He stopped again at the door and lifted his hand. The old man waved him on, and then he was alone again. The mowers came back. A little later the attendant to lead him away.

He stood in front of the courthouse again, again the

heat and the sulphurous haze in fixed and breathless canopy above the traffic. He took the dollar from his pocket and pressed out the creases between his palms. It would leave him two dollars and what was left of the fifty cents, since he had gotten five and a half for the hides of which, he had paid the two to Sylder and now this dollar which he hadn't even known that he owed. Then he climbed the walk, the dollar in his hand, past the arch and past the tireless bronze soldier and under the new shade of the buckeyes. He mounted the gritty footworn steps upward in a rush, into the hall, turning left and coming again to the long counter with the desks behind it. There was only one woman there, not the one he had traded with before. She was at a typewriter, the machine clacking loudly in the empty room. He stood at the counter watching her. After a while he coughed. She stopped and looked up. Can I help you? she said.

Yesm.

She still sat, hands poised over the machine. He stared back at her. She lowered her hands into her lap, swiveled the chair about to face him. He said no more and she rose and crossed slowly to the counter, adjusting her glasses as she went.

Well, she said, what can I do for you?

It's about the bounty, mam. Hawks.

Oh. You have a hawk. She was looking down at him.

No mam, I done give it to ye. He had the dollar out in his hand now and waving it feebly, wondering could the price have gone up. I was figuring on trading back with ye if you-all don't care, he said.

Her brows pinched up a small purse of flesh between them. Trade back? she said. You mean you want to get the hawk back?

Yesm, he said. If you-all don't care.

When did you bring it in?

He looked to the ceiling, back again. Let's see, he said. I believe it was around in August but it could of been early in September I reckon.

They Lord God, son, the woman said, it wouldn't still be here. Last August? Why . . .

What all do you do with em? he asked, somehow figuring still that they must be kept, must have some value or use commensurate with a dollar other than the fact of their demise.

Burn em in the furnace I would reckon, she said. They sure cain't keep em around here. They might get a little strong after a while, mightn't they?

Burn em? he said. They burn em?

I believe so, she said.

He looked about him vaguely, back to her, still not leaning on or touching the counter. And thow people in jail and beat up on em.

What? she said, leaning forward.

And old men in the crazy house.

Son, I'm busy, now if there was anything else you wanted . . .

He smoothed the dollar in his hand again, made a few tentative thrusts, pushed it finally across the counter to her. Here, he said. It's okay. I cain't take no dollar. I made a mistake, he wadn't for sale. He turned and started for the door.

You, she called. Here! You come back here, you cain't . . .

But that was all he heard, through the door now, running down the long hall toward the wide-flung outer doors where a breeze riffled the posters and notices on the wall and past them and again into the candent May noon.

The boy had already gone when they came from Knoxville, seven years now after the burial and seven months after the cremation, and sifted the ashes, since whipped to a broth by the rains of that spring and now dried again, caked and crusted, sifted them and there found the chalked sticks and shards of bone gray-white and brittle as ash themselves, and the skull, worm-riddled, vermiculate with the tracery of them and hollowed and fired to the weight and tensile cohesiveness of parched cardboard, the caried teeth rattling in their sockets. And a zipper of brass, fused shapeless, thick-coated with a dull green paste.

That was all. They were there four hours, the two officers deferential before the coroner, dusting the pieces with their handkerchiefs and passing them on to him who placed them in a clean bag of white canvas.

Mr Eller bit with his small teeth a piece from his plug of spiced tobacco, refolded the cellophane and put it again into his breast pocket. And the skull, he said. With all the fillins melted out of the teeth.

Okay. And the skull. Johnny Romines stopped, the cigarette half rolled in his left hand and leaking as he gestured with it. So, he said, what I want to know is did the boy know about it or not, and would he know was it his daddy?

I don't know, Mr Eller said. If he did I never heard it. Asides he's been gone off now since May or June and this is the fourth day of August they jest now gettin up there. I figure maybe the old man was the only one that knowed.

Old man Ownby? Was he the one done it?

No, Mr Eller said. Course they liable to thow it off on him to save huntin somebody else.

But he was the one told it?

Near as I can find out he was.

Johnny Romines passed the paper across his tongue and folded it shut. Well, do you reckon it was him? he said.

His daddy you mean? Room for speculatin there too I reckon. Miz Rattner claims that it was and that the boy has gone off to hunt whoever it was put him there. She says it all come to her in a dream—a vision, she called it.

Wonder if she had a vision about him bein wanted in three states, Gifford said.

Mr Eller turned on the constable. No, he said, I doubt she has. I don't reckon she needs any sech either. She's a good Christian woman don't matter who-all she might of been married to and not knowed no better.

The constable looked at the storekeeper.

Or the boy either, Mr Eller added.

Never you mind about the boy, Gifford said. Me and him is due for a nice little talk anyway.

Well, you'll have to find him first.

Wonder who it was, Johnny Romines said. That put him in there I mean. Reckon it was somebody from around here?

I doubt it was somebody from New York City, the constable said. He turned to Mr Eller. And what about that fancy plate he was supposed to have? In his head from the war.

What about it?

Well, they wadn't none. How's she account for that?

I don't reckon she ever thought to ast about it. She jest never would of doubted or wondered about it in the first place. About whether he had one, if he said he did, or about whether that was him in that dittybag if she'd decided that it was either one. Mr Eller rolled his cheeks and spat soundlessly across the constable's bow and into a coffeecan. Seems like you ought to tell your sidekick about it though, he said.

Who's that?

Legwater.

He ain't my sidekick, Gifford said. And I don't have to tell nobody nothin cept as I see fit.

Mr Eller studied a passing fly, apparently ruminating on some obscure problem in the dynamics of flight. Well, he said agreeably, I reckon you're right. Keep him out of mischief anyhow.

Gifford's eyes narrowed suspiciously. What? What will?

Campin up on the mountain. With his shovel and his winderscreen.

Some coughs went their rounds. A milkcase settled floorward creakily.

Humph, said Gifford, unleaning from the counter

with studied ease. He fingered cigarettes deftly from one straining pocket. Then: What's he doin up there?

Mr Eller waited while the match rocketed across the counter. Then he said: Huntin platymum I reckon. Lessen he's siftin them ashes for to make soap.

Legwater was on the mountain three days before anyone could get close enough to him to tell him it wasn't so, that the man never had any platinum in his head and that he was wasting his time, it was all a mistake. The first night he built his fire and was sitting by it with his shotgun leaning against a tree and was sipping coffee from a canteen cup when the hound staggered into the clearing on the far side of the fire and stood with his blind head swinging back and forth like a bear's, muzzle up to catch what clue the wind might bring.

Ha! cried Legwater, leaping up, the coffee flying. Ha! he said, stepped to the tree and snatched up the shotgun. But before he could get a proper sight the dog was gone again, absorbed quietly into the darkness. Legwater leveled the gun at the night and fired, listened after the compounding echoes of the shot for a long time and then stepped to the fire and got the cup and poured it full from the pot, squatting, the shotgun leaning against his knee. He listened some more, but could make nothing out. He set the pot back on the little circle of stones he had constructed and tried the hot rim of the cup against his lip. The hound did not reappear. When he had finished the coffee he rolled his blankets out, reloaded the empty chamber of the gun and settled for sleep.

Toward early morning he woke, sat up quickly and looked about him. It was still dark and the fire had long since died, still dark and quiet with that silence that seems to be of itself listening, an astral quiet where planets collide soundlessly, beyond the auricular dimension altogether. He listened. Above the black ranks of trees the midsummer sky arched cloudless and coldly starred. He lay back and stared at it and after a while he slept.

When he woke again the sun was up. He was still lying on his back and now in the depthless blue void above him a hawk wheeled. He got to his feet and began to walk around, feeling stiff and poorly rested. He scouted in the woods and came back with a load of dead limbs, snapped them to length under his foot and soon had a fire going and coffee warming. When it had perked he sat blowing at a cupful and shifting it from hand to hand as it got too hot or he found a new mosquito bite to scratch at. There was an army rucksack hanging from the tree near his blankets and from the pocket he took some cold biscuits and ate them. Then he got to work.

The ashes in the pit were better than a foot deep and the ground all about was strewn with them. He worked all day, shoveling out piles of ash and then climbing from the pit to sift them with his window-screen. Late in the afternoon some boys came into the clearing and stood for a time watching him. He kept at it, the clouds of ash billowing up out of the pit. Before long they began to comment. He looked at them sharply, not stopping, sifting the ashes, examining charred bits of cedar wood. Soon they were giggling among themselves. He ignored them, adopting an official air about his work. It was no good.

Might be gold teeth too, one of them sang out. A flurry of titters surged and died. Legwater stood up and glared at them. They were five, standing together just at the edge of the trees with grinning faces. He climbed back into the pit with his shovel. From time to time he would stretch his head up over the top of the hole to see what they were about, but about the third time one of them gobbled like a turkey and they all howled with laughter so he gave it up and tried not to look their way. He kept at his shoveling. After a while he heard something clatter near the pit. He looked up and the boys had gone. Then an apple dropped into the ashes at his feet with a soft puff. He stopped and craned his neck up. Sure enough, here came another. He marked its course, leaped out of the pit and seizing the shotgun as he went began a fast walk in the direction from which the apple had come. Brush began crashing. A voice called: Run, fellers, run! He'll shoot ye down and scalp ye. Another: You got silver in your teeth you're a dead'n. He stopped. The sounds died away. On the road further down the mountain high laughter, catcalls. He went back to work. By nightfall he was a feathery gray effigy—face, hair and clothing a single color. He spat gobs of streaky gray phlegm. Even the trees near the pit had begun to take on a pale and weathered look.

The hound came back after dark. He could hear it padding in the leaves, stop, shuffle again. He had eaten the last of what food he had brought and could hardly sleep for the cramping in his belly. He held the shotgun and waited for the hound to enter the firelight. It did not. Finally he went to sleep with the shotgun lying across his lap. He was very tired.

When he went to the pit the following morning the first thing he saw was an old goatskull, the brainpan crammed with tinfoil. He pitched it away in disgust and fell to shoveling.

By late in the afternoon his hunger had subsided and he had cleared the pit so that in one end the bare concrete was visible, blackened and encrusted with an indefinable burnt substance that scaled away under the shovel and showed green beneath.

He was shoveling faster, approaching desperation as the residue of unsifted ashes diminished, when Gifford showed up, badly winded from his climb up the mountain. Legwater stopped and watched him come across the little clearing, his shoes weighted with clay, his face inflamed with a red scowl. When he got to the pit Legwater leaned on the shovel and looked up at him. Well, he said, you want shares I reckon? After I done . . .

Idjit, Gifford said. Goddamn, what a idjit. He was standing on the concrete rim now looking down at the humane officer gaunt and fantastically powdered with ash, and looking at the great heaps of ashes and the screen, the bedroll, rucksack, shotgun.

You think so? Legwater said.

I know so. He wadn't no war hero. It ain't for sure it was even him, but if it was he never had no—no thing in his head.

I'll be the jedge of that, Legwater said, bending with his shovel.

Gifford watched him, moving around to the upwind side to keep clear of the dust. In a few minutes the humane officer leaped from the pit and began shoveling the new ashes onto the screen, then shaking it back and forth to sift them through, a fevered look in his eye like some wild spodomantic sage divining in driven haste the fate of whole galaxies against their imminent ruin. The constable lit a cigarette and leaned back against the tree.

Legwater threw out two more piles of ash and sifted them and then when he disappeared into the pit again Gifford could hear him scraping around but not shoveling. He ventured over and peered in. Legwater was on hands and knees, going over the scraped floor of the pit carefully, scratching here and there with the tip of the shovel. Finally he stopped and looked up. The little bastard was lyin, he said. He got it his ownself, the lyin little son of a bitch.

Let's go, Earl.

His own daddy, the humane officer was saying.

Gifford started toward the road with long disgusted strides. When he got to the apple trees he turned and looked back. Legwater was standing in the pit, just his head showing, staring vacantly.

Well, said the constable.

He kept staring.

Hey! Gifford called.

Legwater turned his head to give him a dumb look, the incredulous and empty expression common to victims of tragedy, disaster and loss.

You want a ride or not?

He pulled himself from the pit and began walking toward the constable, then he was hurrying, loping along, the shovel still in his hand and bouncing behind him. Gifford let him get all the way to him before he sent him back after the shotgun and the camping gear.

They went down the orchard road together, their steps padding in the red dust, the constable swaggering slightly as he did and the humane officer, haggard-looking, his black and sleepless eyes all but smoking, grimly apparitional with the shotgun and the spade dangling one at either side from his gaunt claws. Gifford carried the other's rucksack and blanket roll with light effort and from time to time he sidled his eyes to study Legwater with pity, or with contempt. Neither spoke until they saw the dog and that was very near to the pike, on the last turn above the gate. They had overtaken it and even in the few minutes in which he was allowed to watch it alive Gifford was struck by its behavior. It was walking in the wheelruts with an exotic delicacy, like a trained dog on a rope, and holding its head so far back, its nose near perpendicular, that Gifford looked up instinctively to see what threat might be materializing out of the sky. The shovel bounced in the road with a dull bong and when he turned it was in time only to see Legwater recoil under the shotgun and to recoil himself as the muzzleblast roared in his ears. He spun and saw the dog lurch forward, still holding up its head, slew sideways and fold up in the dust of the road.

The few small windows were glassless but for a jagged side or corner still wedged in the handmade sashes. The roofshakes lay in windrows on the broad loft floors and this house housed only the winds.

Dervishes of leaves rattled across the yard and in the wind the oaks dipped and creaked, and in the wind even the spavined house hung between the stone chimneys seemed to give a little. The doors stood open and wind scurried in the parlor, riffled the drift leaves on the kitchen floor and stirred the cobwebbed window corners. He did not go to the loft. The lower rooms were dusty and barren and but for some half-familiar rags of clothes altogether strange. He came back into the yard and sat quietly for a while beneath one of the trees. Watched a waterbird skim beneath the shadowline of the mountain, cupped wings catching the slant light of the sun, then holding the wide curve in a wingset sweep low over the trees to the pond, homing to the warm black waters. He watched it down. What caught his ear? The high thin whicker of a feather, a shadow passing, nothing. Light was breaking in thin reefs through the clouds shelved darkly up the west. Old dry leaves rattled frail and withered as old voices, trailed stiffly down, rocking like thinworn shells downward through seawater, or spun, curling ancient parchments on which no message at all appeared.

Young Rattner finished his cigarette and went back out to the road. An aged Negro passed high on the seat of a wagon, dozing to the chop of the half-shod mule-hooves on the buckled asphalt. About him the tall wheels veered and dished in the erratic parabolas of spun coins unspinning as if not attached to the wagon at all but merely rolling there in that quadratic symmetry by pure chance. He crossed the road to give them leeway and they swung by slowly, laboriously, as if under the weight of some singular and unreasonable gravity. The ruined and ragged mule, the wagon, the man . . . up the road they wobbled, rattle and squeak of the fellies climbing loose over the spokes . . . shimmered in waves of heat rising from the road, dissolved in a pale and broken image.

He followed along behind, going toward the forks. Once at the top of the hill he paused and looked back and he could see the roof of the house deep-green with moss, or gaping black where patches had caved through. But it was never his house anyway.

Evening. The dead sheathed in the earth's crust and turning the slow diurnal of the earth's wheel, at peace with eclipse, asteroid, the dusty novae, their bones brindled with mold and the celled marrow going to frail stone, turning, their fingers laced with roots, at one with Tut and Agamemnon, with the seed and the unborn.

It was like having your name in the paper, he thought, reading the inscription:

MILDRED YEARWOOD RATTNER
1906 — 1945
If thou afflict them in any wise,
And they cry at all unto me,
I will surely hear their cry.

Exod.

the stone arrogating to itself in these three short years already a gray and timeless aspect, glazed with lichens and nets of small brown runners, the ring of rusted wire leaning awry against it with its stained and crumpled rags of foliage. He reached out and patted the stone softly, a gesture, as if perhaps to conjure up some image, evoke again some allegiance with a name, a place, hallucinated recollections in which faces merged incxtricably, and yet true and fixed; touched it, a carved stone less real than the smell of woodsmoke or the taste of an old man's wine. And he no longer cared to tell which were things done and which dreamt.

His trouser legs were wet and clammy against his ankles. Sitting on the small square of marble he removed one shoe, testing the sock for dampness, resting as any traveler might. From across the tall grass and beyond the ruins of the spiked iron fence came the click of the lightbox at the intersection. A car emerged from the trees at his right and rolled to a stop. There were a man and a woman. She looked at him across the man's shoulder, then turned to the man. They both looked. The box clicked. He waved to them and the man turned, saw the green light and pulled away, the white oval of the woman's face still watching him. So he waved again to her just as the car slid from sight behind a hedgerow, the wheels whisking up a fine spray from the road.

He sat there for a while, rubbing his foot abstractedly, whistling softly to himself. To the west a solid sheet of overcast sped the evening on. Already fireflies were about. He put on his shoe and rose and began moving toward the fence, through the wet grass. The workers had gone, leaving behind their wood-dust and chips, the white face of the stump pooling the last light out of the gathering dusk. The sun broke through the final shelf of clouds and bathed for a moment the dripping trees with blood, tinted the stones a diaphanous wash of color, as if the very air had gone to wine. He passed through the gap in the fence, past the torn iron palings and out to the western road, the rain still mizzling softly and the darkening headlands drawing off the day, heraldic, pennoned in flame, the fleeing minions scattering their shadows in the wake of the sun.

They are gone now. Fled, banished in death or exile, lost, undone. Over the land sun and wind still move to burn and sway the trees, the grasses. No avatar, no scion, no vestige of that people remains. On the lips of the strange race that now dwells there their names are myth, legend, dust.

A father and his son walk alone through burned America. Nothing moves in the ravaged landscape save the ash on the wind. It is cold enough to crack stones, and when the snow falls it is gray. The sky is dark. Their destination is the coast, although they don't know what, if anything, awaits them there. They have nothing; just a pistol to defend themselves against the lawless bands that stalk the road, the clothes they are wearing, a cart of scavenged food—and each other. Awesome in the totality of its vision, *The Road* is an unflinching meditation on the worst and the best that we are capable of: ultimate destructiveness, desperate tenacity, and the tenderness that keeps two people alive in the face of total devastation.

Fiction

ALSO AVAILABLE

All the Pretty Horses
Blood Meridian
Child of God
The Counselor
Outer Dark
The Stonemason
The Sunset Limited
Suttree

VINTAGE INTERNATIONAL
Available wherever books are sold.
vintagebooks.com

ALSO BY

CORMAC MCCARTHY

THE CROSSING

In the late 1930s, sixteen-year-old Billy Parham captures a she-wolf that has been marauding his family's ranch. Instead of killing it, he takes it back to the mountains of Mexico. With that crossing, he begins an arduous and dreamlike journey into a country where men meet like ghosts and violence strikes as suddenly as heat lightning.

Fiction

CITIES OF THE PLAIN

The setting is New Mexico in 1952, where John Grady Cole and Billy Parham are working as ranch hands. To the North lie the proving grounds of Alamogordo; to the South, the twin cities of El Paso and Juárez, Mexico. Their life is made up of trail drives and horse auctions and stories told by campfire light. It is a life that is about to change forever, and John Grady and Billy both know it.

Fiction

NO COUNTRY FOR OLD MEN

In *No Country for Old Men*, Cormac McCarthy simultaneously strips down the American crime novel and broadens its concerns to encompass themes as ancient as the Bible and as bloodily contemporary as this morning's headlines.

Fiction